MASTER OF MAYHEM

The Enchanted Well Series
Book 2

Mary Wine

ARE YOU SIGNED UP FOR DRAGONBLADE'S BLOG?

You'll get the latest news and information on exclusive giveaways, exclusive excerpts, coming releases, sales, free books, cover reveals and more.

Check out our complete list of authors, too!

No spam, no junk. That's a promise!

Sign Up Here

www.dragonbladepublishing.com

Dearest Reader;

Thank you for your support of a small press. At Dragonblade Publishing, we strive to bring you the highest quality Historical Romance from some of the best authors in the business. Without your support, there is no 'us', so we sincerely hope you adore these stories and find some new favorite authors along the way.

Happy Reading!

CEO, Dragonblade Publishing

Additional Dragonblade books by Author Mary Wine

The Enchanted Well Series
Laird of Misrule (Book 1)
Master of Mayhem (Book 2)
Once Upon an Enchanted Well (Novella)

Highland Rogues Series
The Highlander's Demand (Book 1)
The Highlander's Destiny (Book 2)
The Highlander's Captive (Book 3)
The Highlander's Promise (Book 4)

Also from Mary Wine
Midnight Flame (Novella)

Foreword

The times are challenging—

The Eight Years War, or the War of Rough Wooing, was started by Henry VIII who wanted to prevent an alliance between France and Scotland. This union would have afforded the French access to Scotland, from where they could launch an invasion into England. Early in the conflict, the Scottish king died, passing the crown to his newborn daughter, Mary Stuart.

Scotland had a choice to make between a French marriage alliance and an English one. The core of this disagreement was the matter of religion between the Church of Rome and the newly formed Church of England. Between 1544 and 1550, much of lowland Scotland was occupied by English troops intent on finding the baby queen to take her to England so she would be raised as a Protestant.

Edinburgh was burned. Numerous other towns suffered this same fate. Scots were forced to become "Assured Men," bound by contract to defend the English marriage. Mary Stuart was smuggled out of Scotland at five years of age and sent to France where she was raised in the Catholic faith.

Peace was restored in 1550, but much blood had been spilt. The topic of religion divides the lowland Scots. Trust will take a long time to be restored.

When Henry VIII's son, Edward, dies without issue, his sister Mary Tudor takes the throne of England in 1553. She ascribes herself to the Church of Rome and begins to enforce a return to this faith. England has been a haven for those who embraced the break with the Catholic Church under Henry VIII. Now, they must recant or flee.

The borderland between England and Scotland are also torn in this battle between faiths. The only stability lies in clan allegiances. Castles offer protection from invading troops, while clansmen man the walls and survey the land to protect their clan members.

CHAPTER ONE

The Borderland, 1555

R UBEN WAITED FOR moonrise while he enjoyed an apple. He'd found it stored in a small, dugout storage bunker in the forest where his fellow Scots had left it for men like him who were riding the borderland. So close to the border, he wouldn't tempt fate by stopping to hunt and cook something to fill his empty belly. Though the skin of the apple was just a tiny bit wrinkled, it tasted sweet, even after a long winter.

Ruben finished off the apple before he emerged from the forest surrounding the Midnight Well. He slid off the back of his horse and gave the animal a pat on its neck, still savoring the taste of the fruit on his lips. The horse made a low sound before walking closer to the well.

"Thirsty?" Ruben asked jovially. "I am as well."

He pushed the cover that sat on top of the well halfway across its opening. The scent of fresh water rose up to tease him and his horse. The animal pawed at the ground and snorted some more.

"I'm getting to it," Ruben assured his mount.

He dropped the bucket down, heard it splash when it hit the surface of the water, and then he began pulling on the rope. Getting the water back up the well was the part that required some strength.

Ruben pulled hard, smiling when the bucket came into view

with water shimmering inside it. He leaned over to grab it by the side, hoisting it up on one side. The bucket tipped, allowing some of the water to trickle out over the rim. Ruben saw the water droplets beading up as they fell back into the dark well, but there was something else. On the surface of the water, there was a reflection.

Ruben narrowed his eyes, trying to identify what he was seeing. The water stilled in the bucket, his hand frozen on its rim. The water went as smooth as a polished glass mirror affording him a flawless reflection of a girl's face.

He was instantly mesmerized.

No single feature stood out. She was simply dressed, and some would have labeled her plain, but Ruben felt as though a beam of moon light had broken through the veil of night to illuminate the reflection just so that he would always see her face. It was as though the divine hand of some ancient goddess guided its path.

Something snapped. Ruben dropped the bucket, breaking free of the strange enchantment that had rendered him in a trance like state, instead of realizing there was someone on the other side of the well. He jumped back, readying himself for a fight.

The girl gasped, shuffling back a few paces. Her eyes had gone wide in her face, making him instantly feel guilty for frightening her.

"Forgive me, lass." Ruben made an effort to sooth her. He'd never been so sincere or worried that his apology wouldn't be trusted.

"I did not see you, sir," she muttered. "Until I was too close."

And he hadn't heard her. Ruben would chastise himself later for failing to hear the lass approaching. Letting his guard down was a good way to end up dead. For the moment though, he was far too captivated by her.

And tongue-tied.

His horse snorted once again. The girl looked at the animal and smiled.

"Your horse is thirsty," she muttered. The girl pushed the cover of the well back toward Ruben. She reached for the rope that was tied around a beam above the opening of the well. She began to pull the bucket up.

"Let me do that, lass," Ruben said as he reached for the rope but only managed to grasp her fingers because she didn't release it.

Something felt as if it jumped between them.

Some sensation that felt too jolting to be real.

And yet, Ruben knew that she was not some mythical creature roaming the forest beneath the moonlight. Nor had he drunk too much cider. Whatever passed between them, she felt it as well, quickly withdrawing her fingers and clasping them against her chest while she blinked.

"Who are ye, lass?" he asked.

"I am Modesty Hawlyn."

Her name sunk in, helping Ruben to resume thinking. "Yer sister Braylin sent me here."

"My sister?" Modesty questioned.

Ruben nodded. The bucket was once more at the top of the well. He lifted it up and placed it on the ground so that his horse might at last have the drink the animal craved.

"Aye." Ruben reached into his jerkin. "Braylin has sent ye a letter. I promised to bring it to ye."

"Braylin," Modesty whispered the name almost reverently.

She hurried around the well, not stopping until she was within a hair's breath of him. Ruben was fascinated by her. So much so that he failed to release the letter when she attempted to tug it from his fingers. A little furrow appeared in the center of her forehead in response.

"Apologies, lass," Ruben regained his senses. She succeeded in pulling the folded and sealed parchment free, the corners of her lips rising once more.

Her smile was more pleasing than anything he'd ever seen.

"Modesty?"

Someone was calling from down the hill.

"You must go." Modesty forgot the letter and looked at him. "My brothers will raise the alarm and you are Scot."

Whoever was looking for her called again. Ruben reached up and tugged on the corner of his cap.

"I am Ruben Lindsey, lass." He'd never wanted a lass to know his name so much before. Ruben locked gazes with her, needing her to realize how important the introduction was to him.

She shivered. Or maybe the better word was trembled. Ruben noted the delicate ripple that moved down her frame. She hugged herself, her eyes widening before she shook her head and retreated a pace.

"Well…yes…Scots…so hurry on your way please. I do not care to see you drug into the market square over stopping to water your horse."

Ruben was tempted to stay right there. But in her eyes, there was true concern. If he stayed, he'd be risking more than his own suffering, and for once, that mattered to him.

"Until next we meet, lass."

"Oh, we can never meet again." Modesty scolded him softly. "Please stay well away from here. There is a new garrison of soldiers here to secure the border. They might convict you of being a spy." She extended her arm, pointing behind him. "Go, sir, and be careful. This is not a safe place."

Her voice rang with a note of fear edging it. Ruben felt his body tighten in response.

"Braylin says yer father is devoted to his Puritan faith," Ruben said.

"He is," Modesty confirmed.

"Any garrison sent by the queen would also be intent on enforcing the return to the Catholic Church."

Fear drew her features tight. "My father says we must remain faithful to the Puritan path."

Ruben extended his hand out. "Come with me, lass."

He was mad to make such an offer, and yet, there was no

stopping the words. Even knowing how insane he sounded, Ruben didn't regret speaking.

She started to reach for his hand. Ruben knew he didn't imagine it. But her name came from down the hill again and she turned and started running toward whoever was searching for her.

Ruben had never been so close to tossing a lass over his shoulder in his life.

He clenched his jaw against the impulse. Aye, he was Scots, but that did not mean he was lawless. Or without honor. The lass was gone, back to her family. Such was a natural thing.

Yet he wished she'd put her hand into his.

"*Until next we meet, lass.*"

Modesty hurried down the path with Ruben Lindsey's voice echoing inside of her head. Her brother James was standing there where he could still see the house they lived in. At seven winters, James wouldn't venture further. He stood there at the top of the yard, looking into the darkness for her, while holding onto an imaginary apron string that was firmly attached to the house.

The darkness was something he feared still. Their parents had certainly done their best to instill that fear into her too.

But the night sang to her.

While her parents and brothers were stuffing up their ears with wool and shutting themselves in during the dark hours, Modesty snuck out to hear the night wind and soak up the moonlight. Under the cover of darkness, she could at last be at ease. Free from her parents' strict Puritan beliefs.

She loved her parents, truly she did.

You do not like being called Modesty...

The small voice in her head rang true. When her father had turned to the Puritan faith in his quest to have sons, he'd renamed all three of his daughters after virtues he advised them to devote themselves to embodying.

Now she was known as Modesty. Her sisters were Prudence and Temperance. Yet she recalled a time when her sisters had been Anne and Braylin and she had been Sabine.

The letter was tucked securely inside of her sleeve. Modesty felt heat stinging her cheeks. It was a blush born of pure guilt sure enough. She'd been so awe struck by Ruben Lindsey, the first news from her sister Prudence had simply slipped off her mind.

Ruben had called Prudence, Braylin.

Modesty smiled. Her lips simply curled up until her lips parted in response to how happy she was. No, she had no idea what words the letter held but there was news, when there had been nothing but silence for months upon end since her sister had been taken away by Scots.

Long months, during which Modesty had feared the worst concerning her sister's fate. Really, Modesty should feel ashamed for being interested in anything beyond the letter. How could she be so captivated by the messenger?

Ruben Lindsey's face filled her mind again. She hadn't meant to think of him. It simply happened and now that it had, she felt the heat on her cheeks spreading down her body. Where their hands had so very briefly touched, it felt as though the skin was on fire.

How much more intense would that sensation be if she'd taken his invitation and placed her hand into his? Temptation needled her, encouraging her to turn her head and look back up the path to see if perhaps he might still be there.

Perhaps she should go to him.

"Mother said you should sleep early, so your eyes do not have dark circles beneath them at your wedding," James said.

Her wedding. For a few precious moments she'd forgotten about the match her father had arranged for her. Now that spring was beginning, a date would surely be set for her to take her vows. She had met her groom only for the briefest of moments. His face didn't linger in her mind like Ruben Lindsey's did.

Modesty lost the battle not to look back up toward the meadow. The clouds shifted, allowing the starlight to cast the area in glittering light. Up at the top stood the well.

The Midnight Well.

She'd forgotten about the enchantment!

On the very edge of the English border, the locals told a tale of the Midnight Well being enchanted. If you ate a piece of forest fruit and looked into the water on the night of a full moon, you would see the face of your soul mate.

Prudence had gone up and tested the myth.

The clouds shifted again, revealing a bright, full moon in the night sky. Modesty felt her breath catch.

Had she just met her soul mate?

All of a sudden, her heart was racing, sending blood speeding through her veins. She was breathless, and the feeling was beyond anything she'd ever experienced.

"Modesty?" James reached out and tugged on her skirt to get her attention. "Did you gasp because you are nervous about getting married?"

She'd forgotten James. His eyes were wide in his young face. But he was taking note of every expression crossing her face.

Modesty shook her head, but it wasn't enough to dispel Ruben's face. The memory was so powerful, she felt as though she was looking at a portrait of him.

Such was foolish nonsense. People did not form such strong connections in a mere moment.

And yet, Modesty looked away from James again, returning her gaze to where the Midnight Well was standing so silently at the top of the clearing.

She had not eaten any forest fruit. Nor had she looked into the water of the well. Modesty gasped again when realization dawned on her.

Ruben had drawn the bucket up with the water. Had he eaten forest fruit, perhaps?

The back door of the house opened. Her mother stood there,

illuminated by the fire in the hearth.

"Come in quickly! The moon is full tonight. There will no doubt be pagan rituals and spells cast by those intent on walking a path apart from God."

James gripped a handful of Modesty's skirts, pulling her toward the open door. The warmth of the fire should have beckoned to her, but Modesty discovered herself far more tempted by the moonlight and the possibility of discovering Ruben Lindsey still lingering in the shadows.

Would she put her hand into his if given the chance again?

Indecision tore through her. The letter inside her sleeve was proof of the price she'd pay if she did take Ruben's invitation. It would cost her the family waiting for her inside the little house. Modesty started forward at James's urging but what kept her moving was the certain knowledge that Prudence would never return to the family home.

She knew naught of Ruben Lindsey. What sort of folly would it be to trade her family for the unknown?

It would be exciting…

That little voice inside of her head was trying to tempt her again. Modesty picked up her feet and moved faster. Girls who went into the forest with men often ended up ruined. Afterwards, they found themselves with no other place to go than a house of ill repute.

But, Ruben Lindsey was a man of honor.

Perhaps it was folly to think such a thing without any evidence, but Modesty was sure she felt it. For her, it was as firm as the ground beneath her feet.

Her mother shut the door firmly behind her, the sound making Modesty jump. All of the window shutters were already closed and barred. The scent of supper mixed with the warmth from the hearth promised Modesty the simple comforts of home. It was a far safer choice than the invitation Ruben Lindsey had offered.

So why did she feel so disappointed?

⇶⇷

RUBEN WATCHED MODESTY on her way down to the house.

Why had he offered her his hand?

He was perplexed by the impulse, and doubly so by the fact that he'd been unable to master it before he had spoken the words.

A man lived by his word.

Such was a principle deeply ingrained in him. He didn't lament it either, for honor was something he held in the highest esteem.

Yet he was still staring at Modesty Hawlyn. An English, Puritan girl who had a match made for her just as Ruben had one too. There was a mountain of reasons why he should turn his back and ride away.

Yet he lingered.

There was a soft chuckle from behind him.

Ruben turned to see an old woman. She grinned widely, showing off her gap-toothed smile.

"You saw her in the water…," the woman declared as she pointed at the moon that was now rising above the treetops. "In the light of the full moon….if you eat the fruit of the forest, and look into the water of the Midnight Well, you will see the face of your soulmate."

His lips were still sweet with the juice of the fruit. Ruben shook his head and the crone cackled again.

"Ye should not sneak up on a man, old woman," Ruben chastised her. "These woods are disputed land."

"I know it well," the woman exclaimed. "For I have lived many, many more years than ye have. Here in this place that kings try to claim, but they are too far away to keep a grip on those who live here."

Ruben grunted. "Aye, well that fact does nae stop the soldiers from spilling blood in these woods. You'd do well to stay away."

"I come to the well on the nights of a full moon." She lifted her face when the wind blew. "Do you feel the warm air returning? Spring is eager to break the grip of winter. The Midnight Well is stirring too. It has awakened something inside of you."

"It is nae enchanted," Ruben scoffed. "That tale was begun by a clansman who was sent to dig the well. After all that labor, he thought of a way to keep everyone else away. It is a story, naught else."

"I knew Peadair. Watched him dig this well when young Rhona lived in that house." She pointed down to where Modesty had gone.

Ruben started to say something to dismiss the woman's recollections, but his tongue suddenly felt dry, unable to produce words. The crone cackled.

"I am Norla. This has been an enchanted place for more years than even I have seen. The Fae folk live here and when the well was dug, the water in its depths flowed with their magic. Peadair was the first man to be enchanted. He spirited young Rhona away. The pair bound by the magic of the well."

Ruben looked back toward the well. He'd heard tales of it his entire life, but he'd dismissed them as clever ways of keeping the English from using the water.

Norla tossed something down at his feet. Ruben looked to see the core of the apple he'd so eagerly consumed.

"Ye saw her face in the water, beneath the full moon. She is yer soul mate. Fail to heed the Midnight Well, and ye will live a life without love."

Norla finished her warning and started back into the forest. The clouds shifted again, covering the moon, almost as if the night itself wanted to help the old woman disappear.

It was nonsense, of course.

So why did Ruben look back down the path Modesty had gone, feeling as though there was a string connecting them?

CHAPTER TWO

MEALS IN THE Hawlyn home were simple. Modesty had never been so grateful for that fact as she was with Prudence's letter concealed inside her sleeve. They would not be lingering at the table. Soon she would be able to seek the privacy of the alcove above the main floor of the house where she and her sister Temperance slept.

Anticipation was bubbling away inside of her. She'd had no reason to think she would ever receive word of her sister's fate, but she had hoped, of course.

And now, she had a letter!

Her parents truly embraced the ideals of the Puritan faith. There was no celebration of feast days or pagan festivals such as Samhain or May Day. Yet Modesty and her sister Prudence had gone to a Samhain bonfire.

It seemed so long ago and yet, it was but one season. Winter never moved quickly like spring or summer did and the last one had dragged on for an eternity because Modesty hadn't known her sister's fate.

Prudence had seen the face of a Scot in the water of the Midnight Well.

It had seemed harmless enough. Just a little whimsy under the full moon. Norla, the old woman who helped in the house, had told them to go up to the well under a full moon and so they had. Modesty had witnessed the way her sister Prudence was captivated by the Scot she met at the well. But seeing it was nothing compared to the way it felt to have her own encounter.

In just the blink of an eye, Modesty had discovered that she had a deep wellspring of feelings inside of her. It was as if she'd been walking around with her eyes closed and suddenly they opened.

She could see Ruben's face still. Sitting there eating a meager meal of porridge without a bit of sugar or dried fruit, Modesty discovered herself fighting the urge to smile at the recollection. He'd unleashed something inside of her. Even if it was a sin, she liked the way he made her feel.

Modesty felt her cheeks warming in spite of the fact that her parents had let the fire die down now that supper was cooked. With spring beginning, there was no need for a fire at night.

"Modesty? You are flush."

Her mother stood up, coming around their small table to lay her hand against Modesty's forehead.

"Do you ache?" her mother asked.

"No," Modesty answered.

Her mother peered intently at her.

"Temperance, you shall sleep down here tonight. If your sister has a fever, I do not want it to spread to you," Master Hawlyn spoke quietly. "Modesty, you are dismissed from evening chores."

Modesty opened her mouth to protest but the letter tucked into her sleeve was more tempting than doing supper dishes. She nodded before stopping in front of her father and knelt down in front of him for his evening blessing.

Her father put his hand on her head. Modesty held still while he muttered a soft, sincere prayer.

"Good night, Modesty."

"Good night, father."

Modesty took a small tin lantern from the table and went up a narrow set of steps to reach the floor above. The spot she slept in was tiny. Just a little section at the end of the floor. The roof slanted on either side of the room but there was a sturdy door to help keep in the warmth from the chimney.

In this small space she could at last be free from the tight cap her father insisted she wear. Modesty had thrown the little linen garment more than once but tonight, she was far more interested in reading the letter.

There was a small stool between the beds. Modesty placed the lantern on it. Made of tin, it had cuts in it to allow the light from the candle out while offering protection from the flame being blown out. Modesty took another look at the door to make sure it was closed before she tugged the letter free and opened it.

My dearest family. I hope this letter will someday find its way to you. Be happy, for I am very well.

Modesty drank in the details of the letter. Prudence was married and happy. Actually, Modesty looked again at the signature on the bottom of the letter. Her sister had signed it Braylin.

Modesty sat for a long moment. Ruben's face rose from her mind while she contemplated her own name from before. Back when the family had celebrated things such as Samhain. Modesty slowly smiled. She and Braylin had gone to a Samhain bonfire just a single season before. It had been a grand time full of frivolity.

But it had led to her sister being taken away by the Scots. A chill raced through her. The winter had been long and bitter with the entire family worried about Braylin's fate.

"Modesty? I have brought you some..."

Her mother didn't knock. She was pushing in the little door while holding a pottery mug in one hand.

"...tea." Her mother's gaze was on the letter.

Her father had decreed that the entire family should be grateful that no blood had been spilled and that Braylin's fate was her own doing for going to the Samhain dance. Modesty had kept her silence, but she disagreed with her sire. A need to know how her mother felt had burned inside of her. Now, there was no quelling the urge to see what was truly in her mother's heart.

"It is a letter from Braylin,," Modesty stated the truth clearly.

Her mother stiffened, her eyes widening. "However did you

come by it?"

"A Scot delivered it to me just after sunset."

Modesty watched her mother's face, intent on seeing her true, first reaction.

Her mother's eyes narrowed but not in disapproval. She tugged the door shut firmly and hurried over to where Modesty sat. Her mother thrust the mug toward her. Modesty barely managed to curl her fingers around it in time before her mother relinquished it and plucked the letter from Modesty's grasp.

Her mother scanned the page, her face tight with fear. There was the truth that had gone unspoken in their house all through the bitter months of winter. Her mother did not love her sons more than her daughters.

"Oh...such happy news."

Her mother looked up suddenly, realizing that she'd been completely absorbed in the letter. Modesty smiled at her mother.

"Of course, I would have preferred that your sister had not been taken away by force. Your father is right to warn us about the dangers of going to such things as bonfires. Your sister has been greatly blessed and delivered by grace."

"She has," Modesty agreed. But Modesty heard the ping of jealousy in her own voice.

And her mother didn't miss it.

"Do not long for such a fate, Modesty," her mother implored her. "It is normal to be nervous about your match. Eleph Cressens is a fine young man, a good son, and strong in faith."

"He said not a single word to me when we met, mother," Modesty spoke softly. "Nor I to him."

Her mother laid a soothing hand on her forearm. "You must trust in your father's judgment."

"As you are trusting that remaining Puritans will not get us all convicted as heretics?"

Her mother sucked in a stiff breath. "Modesty, mind your thoughts. Do not rebel against your parents. Such is a mortal sin."

"Mother, I do not wish to stray from the path of grace, but

are we not bound to obey our queen as well?"

Her mother's face became etched with worry, betraying how much she secretly agreed with Modesty.

"I must respect your father's choice."

"You mean obey," Modesty argued.

Her mother gave her a stern look. "Yes, Modesty, obey. That is the position of a wife. Of women."

Her mother's tone was thick with warning. She stood and started for the door, but she stopped and turned to look back at Modesty.

"To be a woman is to understand that happiness often comes from seeing your home happy." Her mother locked gazes with her. "All men desire sons. It is the duty of a wife to provide them, no matter what is required of her."

Her mother disappeared through the door, closing it softly behind her. Modesty held the simple pottery mug, feeling the way it warmed her fingers.

Her mother found joy in making those around her comfortable.

It was the place of a mother and of a wife, and many would say of a daughter as well. So why did the idea of obedience irritate her so very much?

Modesty truly wished she knew the answer to her question. Instead, all she discovered was an increased longing to read Braylin's letter once more. Her memory offered up the way Braylin had danced in the firelight with the self-proclaimed "Laird of Misrule" at the Samhain bonfire.

Her sister had looked so very happy to be alive.

Much in the same way that Modesty had felt when Ruben appeared at the Midnight Well. A need to skip and dance had pulsed through her because standing still was simply impossible with the way Ruben had set her heart racing. Had she not experienced it herself, Modesty wouldn't have believed such a thing was even possible.

The silent, somber-faced groom Modesty was heading toward

in another two weeks held not even a hint of appeal. None at all!

Lindsey lands—

"IT'S GOOD THAT ye are back, Ruben."

Ruben handed off the reins of his horse to a lad. The boy was lanky but tall. He took the horse away with confidence.

Ruben locked gazes with his father's captain. Arland wasn't welcoming Ruben home with joy. No, the veteran retainer of the Lindsey clan had worry etched into his face.

"There has been a letter from the Douglas," Arland began. "Yer father will not let anyone see it. He's asking for ye, Ruben. He did not care to hear that we had no inkling of where ye had gone. Alone."

There was subtle note of reprimand in Arland's tone.

Ruben locked gazes with Arland. "I should not have given ye cause to worry."

His father was ill.

Ruben avoided admitting that his sire was gravely ill, but there was no way to avoid it when he arrived at his father's bedchamber.

Laird Lindsey had not been out of the chamber in months. Hope was something that had dried up sometime during the winter. Now, Ruben felt his gut tightening as he raised his hand and rapped on the door with his knuckles.

The door opened a moment later. One of the Lindsey retainers looked at Ruben and pulled the door all the way open so Ruben might enter the chamber.

He missed hearing his father call out permission for him to enter. Laird Lindsey was reduced to a shell of his former self now, his booming voice nothing but a memory. All he managed to do was to lift one hand and gesture Ruben forward.

"Father," Ruben greeted his sire. "I am sorry to make ye wait upon me."

His father was laid out on the bed. His body was just skin and bones now. Some manner of disease had him wasting away while his mind was just as keen and sharp as it had always been. A fire was burning in the hearth and there were thick blankets beneath and on top of the laird.

Ruben heard the door shut behind him. He looked over his shoulder to see that the retainer had left.

"The Douglas...the damned Douglas's have broken their word to me," Laird Lindsey declared.

His father began to wheeze.

"Here now, father, there is no reason to be so angry." Ruben tried to sooth his father.

Laird Lindsey growled. "They have broken yer...engagement...gone and promised that girl to the Gordon....the damned Gordons!"

Whatever Ruben might have guessed his father would say, the news surprised him.

"Father, she is but eleven winters old." Ruben tried to calm his father.

"There will be no wedding any time soon."

And he was now, unexpectedly, free of the pledge his father had made. Ruben found himself thinking of Modesty.

His father grunted, recalling Ruben to where he was.

"Aye...well...ye will need a wife much sooner than that lass will be ready," Laird Lindsey agreed. "I agree with ye, Ruben. Better to move on from the girl. Ye are wise to think of ensuring the Lindseys feel yer blood line is secure. A more suitable bride will be found, without us needing to be the ones to break the arrangement."

His father suddenly nodded and smiled at Ruben.

"Ye will be a fine laird for the Lindsey," his father praised him. "Ye do nae let the scheming Douglas get ye fired up."

His father's expression became worried. He looked around

the chamber, his gaze settling on a place where a set of leather-bound books had once occupied a shelf. The wood was darker where the books had sat for so many years.

"Do nae long for them," Ruben said.

His father grunted. "I long for a time when we were nae reduced to selling our finer things. Curse the English and their war of rough wooing! The Lindseys paid a dear price. So many homes and fields burned."

"It is over now, father," Ruben reminded his sire. "The crofts are rebuilt. Every last one. I saw to it myself. We will have a good harvest. Better times are ahead."

Laird Lindsey looked at Ruben. "I am blessed to see ye've grown into a fine man, Ruben." His father swallowed roughly. "I should have found ye a bride that was nae still a child. Forgive me for that, son. The Douglases would have been a strong alliance. I wager the Gordons knew it very well. That's why they stole the girl away. Spring is coming, but not soon enough for me to see the heather bloom one last time."

Ruben heard the sorrow in his father's tone before his eyelids appeared to become heavy. He watched his father battle to stay awake, but he drifted off into sleep a few moments later. Ruben tucked the bedding up around his father's neck before he turned to leave the chamber.

Ruben stopped, looking at the bare shelves. The chamber had naught left but necessities. His father had insisted on everything being sold to pay for the damage the English troops had done. No Lindsey had starved during the last winter. Ruben had seen to his duty to provide for his people.

But the coffers were empty. If the harvest was not plentiful, their luck wouldn't hold through to the next year.

He rode alone because the truth of the matter was, he could not spare a retainer's pay to have one at his back. There were too many in need. English troops had been a pestilence upon his land for over five years. They stole the harvest and burned the villages.

A dowry from the Douglases would have been most welcome but the truth was, Ruben was relieved to hear of the broken engagement.

He should not be pleased. The Lindseys needed the money, and the alliance, his wedding, would have gained them.

But he felt as if he was suddenly free to draw breath without feeling as if his throat was caught in a noose.

Modesty's face rose from his mind. The memory was so crisp and clear, the lass might well have been standing in front of him. And he liked what he saw, that was undeniable. A sensation filled him, one unlike any he could recall ever having before. Warmth filled him, and it made him realize that it had been a very long time since he'd felt anything other than duty.

"What is that smile for?" Arland was waiting for Ruben on the other side of the door.

Ruben blinked. Modesty's face was gone as if Arland had punctured a bubble that Ruben had crawled inside along with his memory.

"My father is dreaming of seeing the heather. I want to get him some," Ruben replied.

"Heather?" Arland tilted his head to one side while he thought. "There is nae any heather blooming just yet."

"I saw some," Ruben stated firmly.

Arland fixed him with a disgruntled look. "Would ye have seen that heather, wherever it was ye were for the past few days?"

"I went to Black Moss Tower to see Dugan Hay," Ruben answered Arland.

Arland snorted. "There would be no heather blooming there, lad."

For just a moment, there was a glint in Arland's eyes that reminded Ruben of a decade past when the veteran retainer had been the one charged with tempering Ruben's youth.

"Aye, well, I took a letter down to Dugan's wife's family," Ruben confessed.

Arland grunted. "The borderlands. And ye rode by yerself."

Ruben became serious. "We do not have the coin for me to

have an escort."

"Ye are the future of the Lindseys." Arland's tone was hard. "The borderlands are uncertain. Losing ye is something we can nae afford."

"Ye trained me well, Arland."

Ruben meant his words as reassuring, but Arland's expression only darkened. "What will happen to yer sister if ye die out there in the borderlands?"

Ruben was instantly serious. He reached out to cup Arland's shoulder. "My sister is too young to become a pawn in the struggle for power. I expect ye to escort her to Hay land where she can finish growing up. Ye gave me yer word to safeguard her, Arland. That is the only way I can see to the defense of our borders."

"Aye, I gave my word to ye and yer father," Arland replied seriously. "And I will keep it, if that's the way things go. I'd rather see ye and a wife standing at the church doors for the baptism of a child that will keep the Lindseys from fighting over who comes next."

Baptism.

That word stuck as Ruben headed back down the passageway. He knew that everyone got married. As the son of the laird, he would wed too. It was simply one of those things that happened to everyone in life. Now that his engagement was broken, Ruben suddenly had a whole different feeling about the topic of his marriage.

And that feeling led him straight back to thinking about Modesty Hawlyn.

Ruben stopped. It actually took some willpower to make himself stop walking toward the stables.

Getting heather for his father was an excuse to see Modesty.

As the next laird of the Lindsey, he had to hold himself to a higher standard. But as he thought about Modesty, Ruben realized he wanted to be his very best for her.

It made no sense. The desire to please her was so deeply

rooted inside of him, he truly needed to rid himself of it.

An enchanted well? It was folly to believe in things such as that, and yet, Ruben couldn't deny that all he wanted to do was climb back into the saddle and head south to where Modesty was.

He needed to be mature enough to deny the impulse. Somehow, he had to find the strength of will to be the man the Lindsey clan could depend on to see them on to a brighter future.

Ruben realized he'd come to a stop at the end of a passageway. He might turn right or left. To his right was his father's study. The desk would likely have other offers for marriage. The Lindsey clan was an old and respected name. Their financial affairs were not common knowledge.

It was his duty to go down to the study and select a bride. Ruben set his jaw, clenching it against the impulse to turn away from what was expected of him.

"Did ye truly see heather blooming?"

Ruben turned with a flare of his kilt. His sister jumped as well.

"Allision lass, I did nae see ye there."

His sister started worrying her lower lip. When he spoke, she smiled, and stopped trying to become part of the wall. At fifteen winters, Allision was growing into a woman, but her mind was still tender.

"Everyone is busy with father," Allision remarked. "I know that is as it should be."

His sister needed a mother. Ruben tightened his resolve to get on with the business of finding a suitable bride.

"Ye are nae a bother, Allision. You are my sister," Ruben reassured her.

Allision brightened. "Could I ask ye...."

Her voice trailed off and her teeth appeared on her lower lip again.

"Ye may ask me anything," Ruben stated firmly. He didn't care for how helpless he felt. Instilling courage in young lads was something he understood how to do. But when it came to his fragile-looking sister, he was completely lost on just how to guide her into adulthood. "Come now, Allision, it is only us here. Ye can be bold and ask what ye please."

Allision appeared to muster her courage. "Could I be with ye when ye give father the heather? I very much want to see joy in his eyes."

Behind his sister Arland slowly shook his head.

But Allision was looking at Ruben with bright anticipation in her eyes.

Christ, it had been a very long time since Ruben had seen such joy on her face, or anyone else's. His father's wasting illness had cast a shadow that was deep and dark inside the walls of the stronghold. Allision was hungry for a life that wasn't about impending death and Ruben realized he was too.

"Aye I will make certain ye hand the heather to father."

Allision clasped her hands together and actually jumped with joy. "I will go to the kitchen and fetch ye some food for the journey!"

Allision was off in a flash of ankles as she skipped off. The sound of her steps was light on the stone floor, bouncing between the walls like butterflies.

Ruben looked at Arland. His father's captain had his hands stubbornly propped onto his hips. His body was rigid but he titled his head to the side before slowly shaking it.

"Go get the heather," Arland grumbled. "I'll see to looking after yer sister."

Something burst inside of Ruben. A sensation so great, he truly wondered if he was about to follow his sister's example and skip through the passageways. He didn't trust his voice to not betray how jubilant he was, so he nodded.

Arland grunted. "Enjoy it, lad. I doubt you'll see another opportunity to ride the night."

CHAPTER THREE

"**M**ODESTY, YOU SHALL go with me today to the market." Modesty wasn't the only one surprised by her father's announcement. The Hawlyn family didn't leave their home very often.

Of course they didn't. They were in hiding.

"Martin?" Modesty's mother questioned her husband in a gentle tone.

Martin Hawlyn placed a gentle hand on his wife's shoulder. "Her dowry is to include a set of silver knitting wires. I believe it best for her to pick them out."

"There might yet be ice on the road," Thomas spoke up.

"Perhaps," Martin Hawlyn answered his eldest son. "Yet the wedding is set for three days hence. We must go today."

"In three days?" Modesty exclaimed.

Her father appeared surprised by her reaction. "The matter has been agreed upon. Spring is the time for weddings. We only wait until after May Day to ensure that we do not bless your union while there is sinful celebration all around you. Tomorrow, the shutters will remain closed lest we hear the pagan sounds carried on the wind. You and your sister must go to the work shed before sunrise and seal the door firmly."

May Day truly was a day of celebration. Girls would wake at dawn to go and wash their faces with morning dew to ensure their beauty. There would be dancing on the green and the Hobby Horse would arrive to help ensure fertility.

To wed on May Day was considered very lucky. It was a double blessing as well for if those girls rounded with new life, it was considered a sign of a good harvest to come.

"Modesty, do not become lost in your thoughts." Her father interrupted her musings. "Have faith that I will place you upon a good path in life."

Modesty nodded her head because she didn't trust her voice to not give away her doubts. Her head was swirling with them.

Modesty went to fetch her surcoat. Spring was only just beginning, and the air was crisp. The sturdy wool garment went over her dress, granting her protection from the wind. She enjoyed the sleeves of the garment. It was much better than a cloak that only secured around the neck and so often choked her.

The ride to the village wasn't long enough to suit her. Modesty was still absorbed in her thoughts when they made it to the edge of town. The pair of horses pulling their cart made it to where the roads were covered in cobble stones. The sound of their steps changed, recalling Modesty to where they were.

Here there were stone buildings. Most rose two stories above the streets. There were signs hanging out, telling everyone what manner of business the shops did. Her father was sitting on the front seat of the cart, instructing his eldest son Thomas on how to drive.

"Here." Martin Hawlyn pointed at a shop.

Thomas pulled on the reins a little too hard, causing the horses to scream in protest. Her father grabbed his son's hands, teaching him the proper amount of strength to use. The team settled down. Martin Hawlyn climbed down and waited for Modesty to join him.

A little brass bell was mounted on the door of the shop. It rang out cheerfully when Martin pushed the door in.

"Good day to you…" The shopkeeper called out a greeting while he turned to face them.

But the smile on the merchant's face faded the moment he recognized them. "You Puritans are not welcome here."

Her father's forehead furrowed. "I traded with you just last summer."

The shopkeeper flattened his hands on the counter. "Aye, you did. Be on your way before anyone notices that your boy is sitting outside my door. I do not need any trouble from the soldiers, you understand. They will be in here asking if I am one of you Puritans."

"I see," Martin Hawlyn remarked.

"It would be best if you did see." The shopkeeper lifted his hands up and held them out. "It's not the way I want it. You understand that? Being out in the country won't protect you forever. The queen is set on every subject being obedient to her will. The soldiers brought a priest with them. It is only a matter of time before it is noticed that you and your family do not come to mass."

"My family will never attend mass," Martin Hawlyn stated firmly.

The shopkeeper backed away from them. "Leave my place! I do not want to hear anything from you! Go!"

Modesty followed her father back out onto the road. Thomas looked at them, clearly surprised to see them emerging from the shop so quickly.

"We will go to another place," Martin Hawlyn announced softly. He was holding onto the side of his short robe, appearing mild and content.

But Modesty saw how white his knuckles were.

Modesty suddenly saw how many people didn't look at them. Strangers were normally a curiosity but today, those out shopping didn't make eye contact. Mothers even warned their children from looking at them.

A chill touched Modesty.

She knew very well that they had fled their home in London because the new queen was a Roman Catholic. Mary Tudor was intent on returning England to her faith. But up on the border-land, it was easy to forget that there was turmoil in the country.

For the first time, Modesty genuinely feared for her family.

The determination on her father's face made it clear that Martin Hawlyn would not go back on his pledge to keep the Puritan faith.

Her groom was a Puritan too.

A sense of foreboding filled her while they moved onto another street and another shop. "Father, I do not need new knitting wires."

Her father was already waiting for her in front of the shop. Modesty found that scooting out of the back of the cart felt as if she was exposing herself to an archer.

"Silver needles would be a vanity," Modesty continued.

Martin Hawlyn was still holding the lapels of his short robe. "Our act of charity so many years ago resulted in you learning to knit. Such a skill is closely guarded by the guilds. Your husband's family intends for you to knit sturdy, warm hats for men from the wool of their sheep. Your fine match is very much attributed to your knitting skills."

Knitting was a new art.

Rare and unique, Modesty had learned it quite by accident. A harsh winter had stranded a merchant and his sons in their home almost a decade past. During the long bitterly cold days, they'd all huddled together in one room to conserve firewood. The merchant's sons had spent that time with slim little needles they called "wires" and used the most basic of spun yarn to knit hats.

A knitted and felted hat might be sold for fifty times what the yarn itself was worth. Like any skill, merchant guilds were quick to keep the secret within their ranks. But Modesty had learned by watching, going up to her room at night to practice what she'd witnessed near the hearth.

"Puritans..." someone sneered at them. "We don't want you here!"

The man who insulted them was driving a wagon. He purposely ventured too close to their cart. The horses snorted and jumped forward. Thomas hadn't been minding them, her brother had been listening to their conversation.

The cart had only two wheels. When the horses lurched forward, the bed of the cart flattened out. Modesty gasped, falling backwards. Thomas shocked into action, fought to bring the them under control.

"Easy…easy!" Thomas called out. He pulled on the reins until the horses calmed and finally stopped.

Her father was out of breath when he reached them. His face was red, but Modesty didn't think it was because of the physical exertion. He was cross with her disobedience and Thomas's inattention.

"Go on!" someone else yelled. "Get ye gone Puritans before we call out the soldiers!"

This time the person sneering at them stood right on the other side of the street. "Old Henry is gone and that little sickly boy of his didn't last either. Know why? Because God wants England back on the righteous path. Our queen is going to have a baby, she is! That's proof that God wants England worshiping the Mother Church!"

"Perhaps it is best that we return home," Martin muttered. He climbed back into the cart and took the reins. A huge clot of muck hit him on the shoulder, splattering onto Modesty.

"Puritans are not welcome here!"

Her father urged the horses on and commanded them to go. Even the animals sensed that they were unwelcome. They took off, their pace brisk. Sitting in the back of the cart, Modesty watched the man who had thrown the mud at them lift his hand and make the sign of the cross over himself as though she and her family were an evil to be feared.

She agreed with him that there was evil at work, but her father's beliefs weren't the cause of it. Hate was. The looks being cast their way made it plain that those who had suffered the loss of their chosen faith during Henry the Eighth's reign were eager to gain revenge now that the situation was reversed.

The feeling of foreboding didn't fade when they left the village behind. Her throat was tight too because she knew without a doubt that their days of going overlooked in their modest little country home were coming to an end.

Soon there would be nowhere for them to hide.

>>><<<

"MODESTY? ARE YOU going to go out and bathe your face with May Day morning dew?"

Temperance asked the question quite some time after Modesty had pinched out the candle in the tin lantern.

The lateness didn't matter. Modesty had had trouble sleeping. Her bed simply wasn't as comfortable as it had been the night before. The little loft had lost its comforting, secure feeling.

"This will be your last May Day to celebrate as a maiden." Temperance continued, "I cannot seem to believe that you are to wed in but two days' time."

Her mind offered up a memory of Eleph Cressens. Her intended groom had sat hunched over in a coat that was two sizes too big for him when Modesty had met him.

Ha! Met was too strong a word!

Not one single word had been spoken between them. Modesty was fairly certain that Eleph hadn't even raised his gaze from the hem of her dress. She honestly wouldn't know if he was the groom who faced her when her wedding day arrived.

Her thoughts drifted to her forbidden messenger. Ruben had introduced himself.

Modesty smiled in the dark chamber. Ruben Lindsey had boldly offered her his hand. She knew it was considered correct for her father to make a match for her, but Modesty just couldn't lie to herself. She far preferred Ruben Lindsey's approach to the way Eleph had stared at the floor.

"Are you holding a grudge against me for telling father about the Samhain bonfire?" Temperance demanded to know. "I only told father about the Samhain bonfire because I was so worried about Prudence. The words simply slipped out."

"I am not holding a grudge," Modesty assured her sister. "My mind is full of other things."

"That's what mother said. That you are worrying when you should trust in father's choice," Temperance said. "But tomorrow is May Day. You don't want to miss it."

She truly didn't. In fact, Modesty felt as if it would be impossible to sleep even a wink for fear of missing out on dawn. The desire to go and dance on the green was raging inside of her. It was far more than just wanting to go. Modesty realized that she was desperate to reach out and grab at any sort of celebration of life because right there in her bed, all she felt was the approach of doom.

"I am going," Modesty said. She didn't whisper, couldn't have lowered her voice even if she'd tried. The need to go was burning so brightly, containing it was impossible.

"Oh good, I truly did not want to go alone."

Temperance whispered. Her voice was low and hushed, but Modesty heard the determination in it anyway. They were both caught in the choices their family had made for them. It felt so unfair. The only thing that gave Modesty solace was the fact that Temperance shared the same frustrations she did.

"We'll go together," Modesty said firmly.

Temperance made a little excited sound that she smothered with her blankets. That little sound was miraculous. It swept through the little alcove like a breeze, carrying away the tension that had plagued the house since they'd come back from the village earlier in the week.

It was a simple thing and yet, hope in any quantity was more powerful than any other force in life.

SCOTSMEN WEREN'T WELCOME in England.

Even if there was peace between their nations at the moment, it was an uneasy truce at best. One Ruben would be a fool to test the limits of by venturing onto English ground.

Ruben recalled where the heather was blooming. It was growing at the top of the meadow where it was afforded more sunlight than the heather that would bloom in the shadow of the forest. Meadows were fine things for they offered a whole season of blossoms.

He stopped before leaving the trees. It was a habit, one that had safeguarded more than one clansman's life. The earthen tones of his kilt helped him to blend in. Even on the borderland, a wise Scot didn't venture into the open.

Ruben stared at the Midnight Well.

It stood quiet and solitary in the night. If he were wise, he'd water his horse, get the heather, and be on his way home before dawn revealed him.

Ruben felt as if his feet had grown roots as deep as the trees around him. Leaving was impossible.

Would she come?

The desire to see Modesty again was like a living, breathing thing inside of him. Standing so close to where they had first met, he discovered himself being pulled back into the intensity of the encounter as if it had happened only an hour before instead of days.

He was playing with fire.

Seeing Modesty again was only going to give him another taste of something he could not ever have.

That thought should have seen Ruben getting on with his business. Instead, he was more determined than ever to linger while grasping at the hope, however faint, that he get one more glimpse of her.

He had a feeling it would be one of the most treasured memories of his life.

CHAPTER FOUR

I T WAS STRANGE the way the forbidden beckoned with such irresistible temptation.

Modesty was up long before the horizon brightened with the first hint of dawn. She opened the single window they had in their loft so that she could peer into the early morning hours and watch May Day arrive.

She didn't want to waste a single second of it.

The wind blew, but this time, instead of the dry sound of bare, frozen branches rustling, there was a softer sound. New spring growth was beginning. There was a chill in the air, but it lacked the bite of winter.

"Is it time?" Temperance muttered still half asleep.

"If we want everyone to believe we've gone to the work shed, we'd best go now before mother and father decide we must keep the doors shut against May Day wickedness," Modesty confirmed.

Temperance didn't need any more encouragement. She was out of bed and straightening the covers in a flash. They both crept down the steps and picked up the bundle of food their mother had left on the table for them.

Modesty collected their shoes before easing the door open while she held her breath and hoped the hinges wouldn't creak. She didn't want her parents to rethink allowing them to go to the shed to work.

Venturing out into the darkness should have been familiar.

The work shed was where the wool was stored. During the long days of winter, Temperance had carded and spun while Modesty knit the newly produced yarn into garments that would be sold or traded.

Leaving before the sun rose was quite normal. Yet today it felt different. Modesty felt the air cool her cheeks. The air smelled wet and new, sparking a sense of new beginnings inside of her. The Celts called this day Beltane. It marked the boundary between fire and ice. Today was the day that life began to flow through the land once more.

She felt it in the wind.

In fact, Modesty would have sworn she could hear the buzz of every living thing waking up after the long winter. It was a feeling that went all the way to her bones.

And she was eager to be a part of it. More than eager really. The truth was, she was desperate to run toward life because she felt as if the shadow of a life that lived inside the dark boundaries of obedience was stretching out its claw like fingers for her.

She had to escape before it claimed her.

They hurried up to the meadow. The horizon hadn't yet turned pink, but the darkness of night was giving way to dawn allowing Modesty to see the Midnight Well. She stopped, staring at it.

"Do you believe the well is enchanted, Modesty?" Temperance asked beside her.

She did.

Modesty bit her lip, determined to not let her sister see her true thoughts. In the gray light of pre-dawn, the odds were in her favor.

"We should take our shoes off," Temperance said.

Her sister sent her a smile full of anticipation. Modesty felt a spark of excitement inside of her. Like the snap of her fingers, it was a sharp, popping sound that let loose a flood of sensation.

She was eager to take her shoes off and indulge in the moment. She felt the dew through her stockings while she worked to unfashion her garters. Tiny little droplets of water soaked into the fabric.

Her skin longed to be free of the endless letters of clothing she wore. It was a bold idea, indulging in removing her clothing.

Oh, but was it rewarded!

When she freed one foot and dropped it down onto the grass so she could work the buckle of her other garter, the dew wet her bare skin. Modesty drew in a stiff breath. Beside her Temperance giggled.

"I have so missed May Day!" Temperance whispered brightly.

Taking time to roll her stockings was just too much to bear. Modesty stuffed them into her shoes and left them beside some heather. The dawn was pink with thick bolts of golden sunlight looking as if they were shooting straight up into heaven.

"Wait for me, Modesty!"

Modesty was already up. The first few steps invigorated her. The meadow was covered in new green grass, appearing so fresh and new. Further up, beyond the boundary of the meadow a gay tune floated on the morning air. Just a flute but it beckoned to them, inviting them to join the others who were up to celebrate the first day of spring.

Temperance caught up with her, clasping her hand before they ran toward the sound of the flute.

RUBEN BLINKED, WONDERING if he was still sleeping.

The sound of the flute continued, filling the dawn with a lively melody. He'd forgotten that it was May Day. He looked at the Midnight Well but decided not to question the gift he'd just received from fate or whatever unseen power was at work.

Modesty and her sister were heading up into the borderland. Skipping along hand in hand to a place where Scots and English mingled freely. He cast one cautious look back toward the house where the girls lived. The shutters were still sealed tight.

The family's Puritan beliefs would keep those shutters firmly latched against the pagan festival the meadows and forest would be filled with for the next few hours.

Which meant he was free to indulge in mayhem with Modesty.

Ruben didn't hesitate further. He set off after the girls. Past the top of the meadow there was a small work shed. The music was clearer here. A drum started up and then a piper joined in.

All around him, Ruben heard the rustling of other people coming through the forest to take part in the springtime festival. Some of them would stop to mop up dew and spread it across their faces. That was a tradition for the younger ones.

A deep pulse of longing would wind itself through those old enough to feel the burn of lust for the fertility ritual. Ruben wouldn't judge them. Life was a mysterious, wonderous thing. Every religion claimed new birth was a blessing from beyond the boundaries of mortality.

He believed it was so.

The shadows and chill that had invaded his home resulted in hunger gnawing on his insides. Nothing could have stopped him from following the sounds of that piper. Tomorrow he would remember that duty was the path he had to walk.

Today he was going to dance upon the green with the woman who had been smiling at him in his dreams.

And the devil could take whoever thought to come between them.

NO ONE SAID they weren't welcome.

Modesty and Temperance found their way to where the musicians were playing. Already dozens and dozens of people were dancing. They offered open hands in invitation, encouraging everyone to join them in the circle. They danced around a huge old oak tree. Lengths of colorful ribbon tapered down from the branches.

The musicians came together and began to play in unison. The music was rich and matched the tempo her heart was pounding in. When the different instruments combined, the sky turned golden.

All the dancers stopped circling. In one motion they danced up toward the trunk of the oak tree, ending up shoulder to shoulder so they might fit. For one moment, they were all sharing the same air, pressing close so that they could feel one another's body heat and then the music swelled, and they went turning and turning and turning in little circles away from the trunk of the tree.

Temperance crumpled down to her knees from being dizzy. Modesty maintained her balance but stopped and laughed as it felt as if her head just kept going round and round. The earth was moist and smelled of early spring flowers.

"You should have your hair down!"

It was a good-natured instruction, hurled out at Modesty and Temperance from a woman who was laughing. She pointed at them.

"Off with those modesty caps!"

Compliance had never come so easily to her. Modesty found the tiny button that secured the chin strap of her skull cap. It popped free, making her feel as if she might draw a deep breath for the first time in a very long time.

Temperance was ahead of her. She'd removed her cap and combed through her hair with her fingers. The drummer started up again, hitting his sticks together to herald the next round of dancing. Everyone grabbed each other's hands. Modesty went with her cap still clinging to her head.

The music was faster now. Sweat trickled down the sides of her face, but Modesty kept up. They danced in one direction and then when the musicians jumped and turned around, the dancers all reversed direction. They crisscrossed their steps to ward off bad luck and raised their faces to the dawn so that light would fill their days with warmth and a good harvest.

But before they all ran back up toward the trunk of the grandfather tree, there was a round of giggles. From somewhere up on the other side of the ring, the Hobby Horse arrived.

A man danced into the ring with the wooden costume of the Hobby Horse on his shoulders. Thick leather straps kept the horse body around his torso and its long neck was out in front of the horse with a small set of ears and a mouth that the wearer could work open and closed with a string. A fabric skirt came down to his waist, but it didn't hide the kilt that he wore.

Modesty gasped. The man himself was wearing a leather mask, but she knew it was Ruben.

"Don't worry, Modesty," Temperance giggled beside her. "You are getting married tomorrow, so the Hobby Horse can nip you this year."

Modesty turned a stunned look toward her sister. Temperance giggled in response. Modesty was still struggling to accept that she was going to become a wife before the week was finished, much less thinking about having her own children. Or creating them.

She looked toward Ruben. Her cheeks grew hotter. Something about him beckoned to her. She just wanted to get closer to him and the impulse was nearly impossible to ignore.

The musicians began to play for the Hobby Horse. For his part, Ruben lifted his knees high, prancing back and forth while he pulled on the string that operated the mouth of the horse.

Snap-snap-snap.

"We need a May queen!"

The May queen was an important symbol. If the girl became pregnant, it was the sign of a good, bountiful harvest to come. The roots of the tradition ran back a millennium. Even if they were all Christians now, the superstition still had very deep roots.

"My sister is getting married tomorrow!" Temperance called

out.

People turned to look toward them, hopeful expressions on their faces.

"It's true," Temperance confirmed.

The crowd needed no further urging. They surrounded Modesty, pushing her forward and standing at her back so that she had no possibility of escape. Her linen cap was gone, and her hair combed out.

"Here, dear," a woman said softy. "A crown of new heather."

The crown was beautiful. Lovely heather blooms were all braided and tied together in a cornet. Modesty bent over so the woman could place it on top of her head.

"There, ye are a fine May queen."

There was a soft hint of Scotland in her tone. There on the borderland, Scots, Welsh, and English all mingled freely as their ancestors had done.

That was why Ruben was there.

Modesty looked toward the Hobby Horse. An insane bubble of happiness felt as if it was lodged inside of her when she took the first step toward him. For just this moment, she was his bride. The May queen and the Hobby Horse would play out the ritual tradition of fertility.

Her steps had never felt so light. Her direction was so very true. Ruben was watching her, their gazes locked. He began to dance toward her, weaving back and forth. The musicians played in time with his steps while the rest of the dancers started up the ring dance again.

Modesty was at the center of it all. Somehow, it was the perfect wedding she'd dreamed of as a girl. Overhead the sky turned blue, the day fully broken. She was excited, happiness bubbling inside of her like a spring creek full of rushing water.

"I protest."

Modesty almost hissed at the newcomer.

There was a snap-snap-snap from the wooden mouth of the Hobby Horse. The sound drew an arrogant chuckle from the man who strode boldly between her and the Hobby Horse. He swept her from head to toe, a glint appearing in his eyes.

"Such a magnificent May queen shouldn't be wasted on a Hobby Horse," he declared.

"I assure ye, boy," Ruben argued, "I do nae plan to waste even a wee bit of her."

The dancers hooted with laughter, enjoying the scarlet play on words. The newcomer stood unperturbed, staring back at Ruben with a confident grin on his lips.

"I am Jasper Hardwin."

Ruben pointed at Jasper. "What ye are is interrupting."

Jasper chuckled. He was arrogant but strangely attractive. Not at all the ugly trait her father had spent many evenings lecturing the family on the ugliness of such a demeanor.

"I disagree....good Horse," Jasper poked more fun at Ruben. "I am doing my best to entice this lovely May queen away from you."

"She will not choose you," Ruben declared.

He shrugged off the wooden frame of the Hobby Horse and tugged the mask off. Modesty saw Jasper's eyes narrow as he took in the wide shoulders that had been hidden from his view.

"Fight for her!"

"Only the champion will win the May queen!"

The revelers called out encouragement to the two men. Temperance was suddenly there, tugging Modesty back a few paces. Her heart felt as if it was in her throat when the two men began to circle one another.

But Ruben winked at her.

Several of the women around her giggled, proving that they'd seen it.

"You've got good luck," one of them whispered. "Two fine bucks fighting over you."

Modesty didn't think it good luck at all. Jasper was a hardened man too. Both had wide shoulders and solid frames. The contest might go to either of them. That idea filled her with dread, for she did not want to belong to Jasper, even for the short time of the May Day celebration.

It was a rejection that seemed to well up from deep inside of her. The intensity of the sensation was almost frightening because it threatened to overwhelm her.

But the men were intent on one another. They took slow, measured steps around each other. Jasper unbuttoned his doublet, stripping it off to reveal his shirt.

The music died away. No matter how lighthearted the challenge had been, everyone watching knew this was a very serious match. One that might end in blood.

CHAPTER FIVE

T HEY CLASHED HARD.

Modesty flinched in response. It was raw and untamed.

Fighting was barbaric, she knew that. But still, there was something inside of her cheering for Ruben. Something that liked knowing he was unwilling to relinquish her to another.

Jasper charged in, trying to lock his arms around Ruben's belly. There was a grunt from Ruben indicating a hard impact, but he twisted to one side and got one of his arms around Jasper's body as well. They were leaning into one another, shoving hard in an effort to push the other over.

Then Jasper suddenly switched tactics. He released Ruben and used his fist in an uppercut that connected with Ruben's jaw. The crowd reacted with sounds of breath being sucked in through their teeth.

Ruben reeled. But he charged back at Jasper, ducking low to hit him in his midsection. Jasper went flying, ending up dumped onto the new spring grass. The crowd cheered.

Jasper wasn't finished. He twisted and flipped over, but Ruben was on him, trying to pin him to the ground. Every second they grappled seemed to last an hour. Modesty was horrified but couldn't have looked away if her life depended upon it.

Their teeth were bared, a primal sort of enjoyment glittering in both men's eyes. They wanted victory, craved it, but there was something about the expression on Ruben's face that sent a chill down Modesty's spine. He was more intent, more determined than Jasper.

There was a crunch and a grunt from Jasper. Modesty blinked. Somehow, Ruben twisted and dropped them both to the ground. It was a hard, bone jarring landing. Jasper was straining, trying to dislodge Ruben but he was pinned.

"All right!" Jasper conceded.

Ruben held him down a few more seconds, ensuring the victory. Around them, people laughed, and the musicians began to play again. Tension lingered in the air until Ruben finally rolled away. He gained his feet with a flash of his bare backside when the pleats of his kilt went swaying.

Heat went coursing through Modesty, settling at last in her belly. It was a shocking sensation. One she wasn't really sure of the meaning of, only that it was deeply sensual.

And centered on Ruben.

He offered his hand to Jasper. Everyone watched intently, waiting to see if Jasper would take it. Conversation died away while Jasper took his time deciding. At last, he stuck his hand out, clasping wrists with Ruben.

Ruben turned toward her, his expression changing instantly. When their gazes locked, Modesty felt as if the world around them receded, leaving them on an island where there was nothing except for one another.

"Claim your May queen!" someone yelled. "May she grow round!"

Modesty blinked, stunned by the scarlet suggestion. People laughed, gripping her arms in some attempt to escort her to the chosen bridegroom. Everyone was pressing in on her, making her feel trapped.

"Back to yer dancing!" Ruben commanded them all.

He didn't wait to see if they complied. Ruben strode toward her, gasping her hand and tugging her away behind him. A cheer went up, but everyone seemed to be happy to allow them to leave. The trapped feeling receded with every step she took away from the oak tree. The music fading into the distance, allowing her to hear the soft brush of their steps against the spring grass.

Ahead of them, there was another tree decorated with ribbons. This was a smaller one with a blanket spread out beneath its branches. Without a doubt it was a bridal chamber for the May queen and her consort.

And Ruben was intent on taking her straight to it.

TEMPERANCE STARTED AFTER her sister.

A hard grip on her forearm stopped her. She whirled around to find Jasper holding her back.

"Let's leave those two to the tradition of being alone," Jasper said firmly.

"It isn't proper," Temperance answered him.

Instead of appearing rebuked, Jasper's expression became one of enjoyment. "But it is the tradition of the morning, is it not, mistress? The rosy hue staining your sister's cheeks says she is very happy with her circumstances."

Modesty was blushing.

And so was she. Temperance caught her breath because Jasper was watching her.

"You, sir, are incorrigible."

Her words pleased him. He performed a very polished reverence.

"That shouldn't please you," Temperance muttered but there was an unmistakable hint of enjoyment in her tone. How strange was that?

"What Rakehell wouldn't enjoy knowing he is performing precisely as the gossips say he always does?"

"Rakehell?" Temperance questioned.

Jasper nodded. "Who am I to argue with the rumors? Or to deprive the court of their zeal for blackening names?"

His tone tightened, hinting at some very deep resentment of

his circumstances.

"Well, you are the one who suffers the bad name," Temperance answered. "If you are innocent..."

"I am no innocent, mistress," Jasper assured her dryly.

He really wasn't and yet, Temperance discovered that she had an impulse to defend him. "I do not believe you are without merit, sir."

His eyes narrowed slightly. For a fleeting moment, she thought she caught a flicker of appreciation in his eyes before he offered her a grin that she recognized as being a façade. One he hid his true emotions behind.

"I doubt you are acquainted with very many Rakehells," Jasper taunted her.

"There is no need to mock me," Temperance said. "You are here, very far away from London, the traditional place for Rakehells."

This time, when his eyes narrowed, it was in contemplation of her. "It would seem you and I have banishment in common."

They did. Temperance felt a new sensation move through her. This one was far more personal, linking her in some strange, mysterious way to Jasper.

She liked that. Being connected to him. But she wasn't sure if she should enjoy the sensation or not. It was strange the way she questioned if it was correct to enjoy the way she felt when there was nothing she might do about it.

Honesty was the best path after all.

So she smiled at Jasper. This time, when his lips curled up in an answering smile, she knew it for a true expression of enjoyment.

One she was proud to have earned from him.

MODESTY PULLED HER hand free from Ruben's grip.

For just a moment, his fingers remained tight around her wrist. On his face, there was an expression of refusal. A little tingle shot down her spine in response, but he released her wrist before Modesty had the chance to think about the sensation.

"Would ye have preferred Jasper?"

Modesty shook her head immediately. Ruben grinned in response.

"That does not mean I approve of your fighting," she was quick to say.

"If ye enjoy the outcome, then ye have no place critiquing the method of getting what ye like," Ruben argued pointedly.

Ruben sat down on the length of wool that was spread out on the ground beneath the decorated limbs of the oak tree. A basket was sitting there with a creamy linen cover. He plucked it off to revel a generous offering of food.

Ruben lifted a mug that was sitting next to the basket. He considered her over the rim of the pottery mug. "I would fight any other man who thought to be here with ye."

He drew a sip off the mug. But he continued to watch her, gauging her reaction.

"You are...challenging me." Modesty decided on the right word after a slight hesitation.

Ruben lowered the mug. "I am daring ye to sit down here beside me."

"Do you think I won't do it because my family is Puritan?" Modesty asked incredulously. Her heart had suddenly started beating faster.

"Yer sister goes by Braylin now, not the Puritan name she left here using," Ruben stated. "What name do ye want me to call ye this fine May Day morning?"

"Sabine."

Modesty spoke without thinking. It had been so long since she'd heard her previous name, it sounded strange even to her. But answering his dare made heat flicker to life inside of her.

"Now that is a fine name, Sabine." Ruben took another sip

from the mug. He sat it down and gestured to her. "Come here, lass. According to yer sister, this is yer last morning of being able to be Sabine."

It was.

Modesty was already on her way onto the blanket before she finished thinking. Perhaps later she would contemplate just why she seemed to be so full of impulses, but not now. She just couldn't bear to squander the opportunity before her.

Tomorrow, Modesty was getting married.

And not to Ruben Lindsey.

That thought made her blush. Without a doubt, she admitted she would feel very differently if her groom were the man grinning at her.

Ruben handed her a mug. "It's fine cider, lass. Someone must have been saving it for this morning."

Sure enough, the cider did indeed have a pleasing scent of fall apples and a hint of spices. Modesty closed her eyes to better appreciate the scent before she lifted it to her lips and drew off a sip.

Ruben chuckled. "Aye, it's worthy of the May queen and her consort."

Modesty's eyes popped open in response to the word consort. She ended up staring straight into Ruben's eyes.

"You shouldn't say such bold things," she muttered.

Ruben scoffed at her. "I am just the way ye like me, lass."

"You are overly bold, sir."

Ruben had started to put a piece of cheese into his mouth. He stopped short, one dark eyebrow arching in response. "Overly bold?"

Modesty nodded firmly.

He put the cheese into his mouth and chewed, clearly thinking. Modesty discovered herself full of anticipation while he decided upon his response to her accusation. Ruben made her wait for what felt like an eternity, taking a long drink from his cider before he pointed at her.

"Bold, now that I agree with, lass. But overly bold...well now, I do nae believe I have crossed that line just yet."

Something glittered in his eyes. A promise of some sort. Modesty was mesmerized by it, so much so that she failed to realize he'd reached for her wrist.

She gasped. He carried her hand toward him, turning it so that the delicate skin of her inner wrist was exposed. She saw that glint in his eyes again before he lowered his gaze and his head. He pressed a soft, slow kiss against her inner wrist while Modesty shuddered.

He felt that reaction. Ruben lifted his head to lock gazes with her once more.

"Now that is overly bold...Sabine."

He released her wrist, returning to the mug of cider. Modesty got her mug to her lips first, tipping it so that cider filled her mouth. Swallowing so much at once was hard and when she lowered the mug, she found Ruben watching her with a little pleased grin on his lips.

"Was that meant as a lesson or a promise?" Modesty was sure she would be old and withered by the time she understood just why she asked such a question. Her cheeks were burning because of her own audacity but she felt more alive than she ever had.

Ruben's expression became serious. He abandoned his lazy position, getting to his feet. He turned and offered her a hand.

Again.

"Come north with me, Sabine." There was a hint of heat in his tone. Somewhere inside of her, she felt a flicker of answering heat.

Modesty's knuckles turned white because she was clenching handfuls of her skirt to keep her hand from his.

"To what end?" she asked. "Surely you have a family with expectations for you and your future. Just as I do."

She didn't want to say those words for it was like she was pinching out a candle. Sentencing herself to darkness.

Ruben lowered himself to one knee next to her. His face was

so close to hers, she felt awareness of him shoot through her body. Never in her life would she have believed she might feel such intensity. His jaw was tight.

Would he kiss her? In his eyes, she saw something flickering. Her belly tightened in response.

Everything about him seemed to draw a response from her. She was completely mesmerized by him.

"Aye. Ye are wiser than I am to think of more than what we both feel now. I am ashamed, for ye are a proper lass."

"You feel it too?"

Ruben grinned. "Aye, lass. The truth is I believe I will remember what ye stir in me for my entire life."

"I will too," she confessed.

The blanket had suddenly become the most sacred of confessionals. Modesty knew without a doubt that she had never bared her soul so very completely to any other person.

He laid his hand along the side of her face. No touch had ever felt so very right or pleased her so completely.

"Forgive me, Sabine, for I cannot resist ye."

She didn't misunderstand his meaning. Modesty knew he was intent on kissing her. The breath in her lungs simply froze while he leaned toward her. The first touch of his lips was soft and warm and more intoxicating than anything she had ever experienced. Her eyes closed shut, clearing the path for her other senses to intensify.

His scent overwhelmed her senses, making her head swim. She reached for him, needing to steady herself. Ruben caught her up against his frame, the kiss deepening. She craved him, needing to be closer. He bound her to him with one strong arm around her back while she reached up and held onto his shoulders.

How long did it go on? Modesty had no idea, only that she was enthralled and happily so.

But everything had to end.

"Go on with ye, lass," Ruben ordered her gruffly. "For if ye stay, I fear we shall both abandon reason."

He was correct.

And she had never loathed the truth so very much before!

Pulling away from him hurt. Every inch of her body protested. Just a few paces and she could see past him to where the little work shed sat. Its shutters still closed tight against the May Day morning frivolity. Ruben turned to see what she was looking at.

"You will not be needing this crown, Sabine."

Ruben lifted the crown of heather and greens off her head. It was a gentle motion, but she let out a little sound of misery for it felt as if he'd taken her very heart. He reached up and tugged on the corner of his bonnet before he disappeared into the thicket.

The wind blew, rushing the limbs of the trees that had yet to sprout with new growth. It was a dry sound, one that heralded a future that was brittle and cold.

HE HAD THE heather, so it was time to leave.

But he couldn't. Instead, he stood in the forest, watching Modesty and her sister go to the shed and disappear inside.

"A little token to remember your May queen?"

Ruben growled at Jasper, but the man had managed to sneak up on him. The Englishman wasn't going to let it go without comment either.

"I do hope that isn't all you claimed from her," Jasper continued.

"Modesty is an innocent lass," Ruben warned Jasper. "Mind how ye speak of her."

Jasper wrinkled his nose. "Modesty…Temperance…horrible names better suited for horse-faced blue stockings. Not at all what I would want to call a girl who kissed you so very sweetly in yon arbor."

"Just remember who she kissed," Ruben said. "It was nae ye."

"I could have fought harder," Jasper argued.

Ruben grunted, making it clear that he didn't agree.

Jasper snorted. "You should thank me. I'm not normally so very accommodating. Not when there is such a sweet prize to claim."

"I'm thinking of thrashing ye again, but yer skull is too thick to recall the first time so…it would be a wasted effort," Ruben said gruffly. "Modesty is a not some lass to be treated lightly. Do nae trifle with her or her sister."

Ruben meant the warning sincerely. He felt the burn of it all the way to his bones.

Jasper turned his head to look at him. "If you care about the girl, you should take her back to Scotland with you."

Ruben felt his insides clench. "Why do ye say that? The girl is set to get married tomorrow. She has a good life ahead of her."

Jasper's expression was dark. "Our queen Mary Tudor has spent a great many years beneath the thumb of those around her. Now that the crown sits on her head, she is intent on ruling with just as much of an iron fist as those who held her fate in their hands in the past."

"Is that why ye are here? So far from the city where yer clothing is more fitting?" Ruben asked directly.

Jasper chuckled. He smoothed a hand along the fine fabric of his doublet. Wool would be more practical, but clothing took time to create, and his wardrobe had been made for court.

"I am in exile like the Hawlyn family," Jasper confirmed. "But I do not see much difference between the faiths, so I am content to be obedient to the queen's decree of returning to the Roman Catholic faith. From what I have seen of Martin Hawlyn, that man will not abandon his faith. Even if it means his life."

Jasper watched his words sink into Ruben.

"Queen Mary has taken matters that far?" Ruben asked.

Jasper nodded. "I believe she is just getting started. The new garrison of soldiers in the village proves how much determination she has. The queen believes she will only bear a heathy male child if God is pleased with her."

Which meant Modesty and her family would soon face the wrath of the queen of England.

Unless he intervened.

Her mother had already lost one daughter to Scotland. Wouldn't he be a scoundrel to take Modesty away?

How much greater would his sin be if he left and heard that Martin Hawlyn had led his entire family to the execution grounds?

"I am grateful to ye, Jasper Hardwin." Ruben offered Jasper his hand. "Ye are welcome on Lindsey land."

Jasper clasped wrists with Ruben.

A moment later he was heading toward the shed. Just how he was going to convince Modesty to come with him, Ruben didn't know. But leaving her behind was impossible now.

CHAPTER SIX

S HE HAD SEEN Ruben for the last time.

An idea had never tormented her so greatly before. It felt as if the knowledge alone was tearing away at her insides with sharp claws. Nausea threatened to send her to the garderobe to retch, while tears stung her eyes.

"You look like you are contemplating breaking down the door, Modesty."

Somehow, Modesty had forgotten that Temperance was there with her. Modesty snapped her attention toward her sister to discover Temperance watching her with wide eyes.

Modesty shot up out of her seat, looking for something to do. Her knitting wires spilled onto the floor. Thin and made of silver, they were pointed on both ends. Temperance immediately stopped working her spinning wheel to help retrieve them.

"You are so fortunate to have such a useful skill," Temperance remarked when she handed over two of the shiny wires. "You have tried to teach me."

"We make a good team." Modesty tried to soothe her sister, but it only made her return to thinking about the fact that she was leaving tomorrow.

She pushed the knitting wires into her pinned up braids for safekeeping. Settling down to begin knitting seemed impossible. The wires were slim, requiring her to pay close attention to the little loops or see her efforts wasted when it became a mess. The pitcher they used for water caught her eye.

"I will go and draw some fresh water."

Temperance had sat back down at the spinning wheel. She had a handful of carded wool in her fingers that looked like a cloud she'd plucked from the sky. She began to work the foot pedals to begin spinning. The spindle spun, twisting the wool thread while Temperance gently plucked and fed bits of the fluffy wool into the line of new thread.

"That would be nice," Temperance replied, her attention on her spinning.

Opening the door of the shed relieved some of the tension knotting up the muscles of her neck. Modesty closed it behind her to keep the warmth in. Spring was so very new, the air fresh and clean but it was still crisp. The shed didn't have a hearth for warmth.

The pitcher was earthenware. Modesty hugged it tight. On the other side of the house sat the well the family used. She stared down at the house with its shutters so tightly shut, even well into the morning. It felt as if that noose was tightening around her neck again.

She didn't want to go down to the house. She didn't want to let fear close around her like a cloak. All around her life was budding. The desire to be a part of it was flickering inside of her, making her realize how dark her existence had been.

But her wedding was planned. The rest of her life had already been decided. She turned her back on the house, finding it to be the only way she could breathe.

The Midnight Well was all the way across the open space at the top. Her sister Braylin had gone up there and looked into the water beneath a full moon to see the face of her true love. Maybe it was foolish to believe in enchantments, but Modesty turned and started toward the well because she just couldn't make herself turn her back on enjoying the fine spring morning.

Tomorrow would arrive soon enough.

Today, well today there was birdsong to listen to. Modesty smiled on her way across the meadow. Near the center of it, where the sunlight didn't have to filter between the branches of the forest trees, there were flowers.

It was like a magical fae glen. One moment she was walking through dry, dead grass bent over from the winter snow and in the next she was treading among new blossoms. Pink, purple, white, and yellow. She was careful where she put her feet down, not wanting to trample the new blooms.

The birds suddenly stopped chattering.

Modesty looked up, horrified to see two men wearing the uniform of the queen's soldiers standing near the well. They were rough and unkempt, but the coat of Mary Tudor was clear on their cassocks. One of them grinned at her, showing off yellow teeth.

"Looks like we're going to get a taste of the May queen herself," one of them declared gleefully. He began to rub his hands together, his eye glittering with appreciation.

Modesty clamped her jaw tight against an involuntary scream. Temperance would come to investigate if she heard her.

She must safeguard her sister.

"Do not trifle with me." Modesty fought to keep her rising fear from her voice. "I will report you."

"No, you will not," the first one said. He was edging toward her. "You will do everything I demand of you..." he pointed past her at the house, "or I will be back with shackles for your Puritan family."

His comrade snickered sickeningly. "The queen has issued a decree. It's our duty to bring in the traitors."

"My family are not traitors." Modesty attempted to appeal to them. She shifted, taking a few quick steps to keep the well between herself and the men.

The two soldiers shared a look before they split and came at her from both directions.

"Come here to me and maybe you can convince me to forget about the Puritans in yonder house."

He licked his lower lip in anticipation. The gleam in his eyes was most defiantly unholy.

Modesty was horrified. She knew she wasn't the first girl to be offered such a bargain. It disgusted her, but she didn't have time to be emotional.

She must not draw Temperance out of the shed. The need to protect her sister started pounding through her. Modesty realized she was no longer afraid. Now, she was determined. A strange sense of purpose had hold of her. It felt as if something hardened inside of her.

She'd do whatever she must.

Whatever...

The first one lunged at her. Modesty swung the pitcher at him. It made a dull, sickening sound when it collided with his head and broke into several pieces. He went staggering off to the side, his knees folding while he held his head.

"You little bitch!" he growled.

The first man grabbed her arm, yanking her back toward the well. Modesty slammed into it, the hard stone exterior sending pain shooting through her lower back.

The first soldier was on her, his foul breath hitting her in the face. "You're going to pay for that!"

Something snapped inside of her. Modesty felt the need to fight flaring through her like straw catching fire. She reached up, intent on clawing his face when he suddenly went stumbling away from her. She gained a brief look at Ruben's furious face before he turned his back on her to look at the soldier.

"Ye English scum," Ruben growled.

He'd flipped around, placing himself between Modesty and the soldier.

"This is England!" the soldier snarled. "We are the queen's men!"

"What ye are is bastards," Ruben growled.

The soldier got to his feet. He reached down, pulling a knife from the top of his boot. "You won't be the first Scot I've killed!"

The second man joined in, the sunlight flashing off his blade.

Ruben looked between them, but they separated, coming at him from two opposite directions. Time slowed down, tormenting her with seconds that lasted as long as hours during which she saw both men handling their weapons with a confidence that she knew meant that they had killed before.

And they weren't going to be fair, either.

They came at Ruben together. He turned and raised his arm to block a downward strike from one of them. The other took advantage of Ruben's exposed side, swinging his blade.

Modesty stepped between them. She'd grabbed the knitting wires out of her hair and thrust them at the man's unprotected neck. The sharp points combined with the rigidity of the silver meant the thin needles easily punctured the man's skin, sliding deeply into his throat.

His eyes went wide. His lips moved but no words came across them. He attempted to thrust his knife toward her and would have found his target, but Ruben grabbed her, yanking her back so that the blade of the knife sliced through the air in front of her.

Ruben kicked out, his foot landing in the man's belly. He fell back, his body contorting.

"Did he cut ye, lass?" Ruben demanded.

Modesty was still staring at the bright red blood coating the man's neck and chest.

"Sabine."

Ruben grasped her shoulders and turned her more toward him. She suddenly recalled the first man and his intention to kill Ruben.

"He was going to kill you," she said.

Whatever he thought of her actions, Ruben suddenly shoved her behind him. Modesty had to lean over and look around his trim middle to see what was in front of them.

Four Scotsmen had been charging down from the top of the meadow. Their faces were flushed with their efforts. They suddenly stopped, huffing and puffing while they tried to regain their breath.

"Christ in heaven, that was too close," one of them declared.

Another made the sign of the cross over himself after looking closely at the one Modesty had killed.

"Arland sent ye after me," Ruben grumbled. He shook his head.

One of the men shrugged. "Aye. The laird is not going to last much longer."

One of his comrades elbowed him in the ribs.

"He knows it well enough, Eachan. No need to jab me over speaking the plain truth."

Eachan was looking at the two bodies. "We should have been closer."

The first man leaned over and pulled the knitting wires free. He wiped them across the dead soldier's clothing before looking at what he held. "What are these, lass?"

Ruben turned sideways so his fellow clansmen could see her. He pointed at the one with the wires. "This is Ardan, Nechtan, and Fintan. Me kin."

They all reached up to tug on the corners of their bonnets when introduced as though there weren't two newly murdered men lying at their feet.

"I didn't think..." Modesty felt as if her throat was already in a noose. She couldn't seem to get any air from her chest into her mouth.

"I am right glad ye took action, lass," Ardan stated.

"As am I," Ruben added.

Modesty jerked her attention back to him. She suddenly needed to see that he was whole and unscathed. "Are you well? Did he cut you?"

Modesty wasn't waiting for Ruben to answer her. She reached right out, flattening her hands on his back to make certain his clothing wasn't wet with blood.

Ruben grunted. He looked at his men.

"Pick them up. Let's toss them into the river and be gone,"

Ruben ordered his men.

There was a solid ring of authority in his voice. The four men didn't hesitate. They split into two teams, hoisting the bodies to begin carrying them back into the forest. They climbed up to the top of the hill, the sound of the river on the other side filling their ears.

Modesty went because she realized she wasn't ready to part from him just yet. A few more moments and she'd be ready to face the reality of what she had done.

She didn't lament it. In all honesty, she could not repent for Ruben's life had hung in the balance. Without a doubt, she knew she would do the same thing again if she might go back a half hour.

"Best to strip the cassocks off them," Arden advised.

A cassock was a full circle garment, designed to fit all sorts of different body types. It made it simple to pull off the men before their bodies were heaved off the top of a ravine. So new into spring, the river at the bottom of the hill was full. The current was fast, quickly swallowing up the bodies.

"Thank you," Modesty said. "I'm grateful to you for not leaving them so close to my family."

"Someone might have witnessed the fight," Ruben informed her gruffly.

Modesty felt a chill shoot down her spine. She swallowed hard, grasping at her composure. "I will face whatever is to come."

Ruben turned his full attention to her. In their brief encounters, she'd somehow failed to recognize just how large and hard he was. With his kin surrounding him, she had little hope of disobeying him. Without a doubt, he was a man with authority.

A ripple went across her skin. A sensation of vulnerability was left behind. The look in Ruben's eyes promised her he was intent on having his way.

"Ye cannot stay here, Sabine. I will not allow ye to shoulder the blame when it was my life ye saved," Ruben told her.

"You were only trying to prevent them from…" She couldn't quite get the word past her lips. Ruben's eyes narrowed.

"God gave me a strong back. I will not shame myself by turning it on those in jeopardy," Ruben declared firmly.

"You are an honorable man, Ruben," Modesty muttered.

He liked her compliment. She saw enjoyment flicker briefly in his eyes before he sent her a stern look. "We must be leaving. Come, lass."

He extended his hand to her. This time, there was a demand in his gaze.

"This is my home," she argued.

Ruben shook his head. "Not anymore."

Modesty tried to recoil but he reached out and captured her wrist. Modesty ended up backing up a pace, her arms stretched out between them because Ruben refused to release her.

"It is May Day morning, Sabine. The forest is full of people," Ruben spoke softly. "I cannot leave ye here to an uncertain fate."

"But no one…cried out," she argued.

"They might be running to alert the other soldiers," Ruben explained. "If ye return to yer home, the soldiers have every reason to arrest your entire family. If ye are gone, they will consider that ye fled rather than face justice. It is the only way to protect yer family."

Modesty shook her head. She tugged on her wrist. For a moment, Ruben held tight but then released her wrist with a grunt. Modesty stumbled back but stopped, realizing she was uncertain as to what to do next.

"My family was not involved," Modesty insisted. "Any witness will know that it was but me and you. And that the soldiers attacked me."

The Scotsmen scoffed at her reasoning. Several of them shaking their heads.

"English soldiers will protect their own," Eachan stated.

"Any witness will say ye started the matter, that Ruben is yer Scottish lover," Arden added.

Modesty blushed scarlet but Ruben had no mercy for her. "Ye were alone with me, Sabine."

She had been. It seemed impossible that everything had become such a mess. "It was just a bit of May Day fun."

Tears flooded her eyes. Controlling them was beyond her. They trickled down her cheeks. Ruben closed the space between them, cupping her face between his large, warm hands.

"It is not yer fault, lass." He tried to sooth her.

"I am not sorry," she declared firmly. "They were evil men. Intent on…on depravity."

"I heard." Ruben's jaw tightened. He swept a last tear off her cheek before he reached down for her wrist again. "Ye must come with us."

"Modesty?"

Temperance was looking out of the door of the work shed. She lifted one hand to shield her eyes from the sun. Ruben closed the distance between them with a quick step.

"Be quiet, lass. Do not bring her into this."

Modesty sent him a disgruntled look. "Why do you think I didn't scream when those soldiers came close?"

Ruben nodded. "That was a fine thing to do. Ye are a good sister."

Temperance scanned the meadow but didn't actually step outside of the work shed. She looked toward the house, likely believing that Modesty had gone down to the well in front of the house and was now inside the house. She shrugged before retreating back inside the shed.

Modesty let out a little sigh of relief.

"Aye, ye are a fine sister, Sabine. I will help ye continue to be so."

Modesty turned to look at Ruben, not understanding what he meant.

She gained only a brief look at his face before he reached out and captured her wrist. He bent over and pulled her to him. Modesty tumbled forward, her belly hitting his shoulder. Ruben lifted her right off her feet, straightening up so that she was hanging over his shoulder like a sack of barley.

"Ruben…" she gasped. "Put me down."

He complied but only after he walked across the ridge and she heard the sound of horses nearby. When he placed her on her feet once more, it was beside a huge, dark-coated stallion.

"Ye are coming with me, Sabine."

He pointed at one of his men. Eachan tossed one of the cassocks. Ruben gave the garment a shake before he grabbed the piece of embroidered fabric on its front and yanked it free. The threads gave with a ripping sound. He lifted it above her head and dropped it down onto her.

Modesty tried to retreat but one of the other men cupped her shoulders, holding her securely in place. Since she hadn't raised her arms to fit them into the sleeve, the heavy wool garment bound her arms against her body. Ruben grabbed the sleeves and tied them tight, securing her.

"Ruben…do not do this," she implored him.

His jaw was tight. "I will not ride away knowing ye could face retribution. It is decided."

Ruben clasped her waist and lifted her up. She gasped at how easily he hefted her weight. She landed in the saddle, and he swung up and onto the back of the horse behind her.

Ruben dug his heels in, and the stallion took off. The animal was eager to be on its way home.

But it wasn't her home, and there was no way to stop him from taking her with him.

CHAPTER SEVEN

S COTLAND WAS AS horrible as Modesty had heard it was.
It seemed that every step the horse took north carried her further into darkness. The sun disappeared, leaving the sky full of thick black clouds. The air became icy, every gust of wind felt as if it cut deeper until her very bones froze.

Thunder began to rumble above them like the belly of some hungry beast.

When the rain came, it was half frozen, pelting every bit of unprotected skin.

Behind her Ruben remained warm. His body adjusted to the temperature while Modesty shivered.

The forest they rode through became ancient. The trees were huge and thick. Modesty didn't know how Ruben and his men were finding their way, for the darkness seemed too thick for her to see through.

But they kept going with a confidence that horrified her because it felt as though they were going through a boundary into another world. One she didn't belong in.

Her first glimpse of the Lindsey stronghold was because of lightning cracking open the darkness. A brilliant flash illuminated three huge stone towers before darkness engulfed her again. Thunder boomed a second later, shaking her all the way to her bones.

"It is only a spring storm, Sabine," Ruben whispered near her ear. "We'll soon be home."

"It is not my home," she argued.

She felt him stiffen. But he continued forward. She heard the horse's hooves begin to tap against more than earth. Now there was a tap-tap-tap like there was something solid beneath their iron shoes. Another flash of lightning illuminated a portcullis. Its iron points were almost directly overhead.

Ruben rode through the gate of his stronghold while a boom of thunder welcomed him home.

Fitting...

Modesty struggled to avoid using a word like terrifying.

She had to be strong. Even when her parents had taken them out of London under the cover of darkness she had never felt so alone.

Ruben was a stranger. One she'd made the mistake of trusting.

Well, she'd been shown just how foolish she'd been for now Ruben was doing what he pleased without regard for her wishes.

On the other side of the portcullis someone opened a door. Light shone out from inside, twinkling like a star. And yet she felt guilty, looking at that light with a spark of hope.

Ruben swung off the back of the stallion and reached back up for her. Going inside was the most reasonable course of action, yet every muscle she had was tight with opposition.

Not that it kept Ruben and his men from sweeping her up the steps and inside the stronghold. It was instantly warmer once they crossed threshold, protected from the icy wind outside.

"It's good that ye are back, Ruben," a man said gruffly. "The laird is weakening. Ye'd best get to his side."

The man looked at Modesty. He swept her from head to toe, taking in the cassock binding her. He looked back toward Ruben for an explanation.

"Wake my sister, Allision. Bring her to the laird's chamber, Arland," Ruben said.

Arland reached up and pulled on the corner of his bonnet. He wanted to know who she was, but he turned and disappeared into the passageway. So late in the night, there were only a few candle lanterns offering meager flickerings of light.

Ruben pulled on the knot in the sleeves of the cassock until Modesty was free. All around them there was naught but shadows. The light from the lanterns flickered. Modesty shivered and it had nothing to do with the temperature.

"Come."

Ruben didn't leave the matter up to her. He captured her wrist and pulled her behind him into the shadows of the passageway.

Into his domain...

It truly was for Ruben strode forward without hesitation. The stone walls were dark and the shadows clinging to them even blacker. He navigated the turns like a wolf who could see in the blackness. He found a staircase and pulled her behind him on his way to the top of it.

She feared if she would ever be able to find her way back to the sunlight.

Maybe that was foolish of her to think but Modesty just couldn't seem to stop her mind from jumping to dramatic conclusions.

How many steps had they taken? She should be counting them if she ever hoped to find her way out of the stronghold. Ruben led her higher and higher and higher. The wind whistled through the archer crosses built into the walls of the tower. She shivered and her teeth began to chatter.

Ruben suddenly stopped. There was the sound of a door opening. Beyond the door was a chamber. There was a small hearth inside of it with a fire burning. The very sight of that fire and the bed nearby was like gaining a glimpse of paradise. Modesty smiled, more appreciative than she had ever been before for the simple comforts of home.

"Stay here, Sabine."

Modesty had started walking toward the hearth. Ruben's grip on her wrist was still firm. He stepped between her and the opening to the stairs they had climbed.

"Stay in this room or I promise ye I will track ye down, storm or no storm. I know my lands."

His features were tight and cut and there was a glint of warning in his eyes. Unlike her, he didn't look beaten down by the cold.

He was formidable.

And a match for the elements that had reduced her to a shivering mess. She wanted to gather her resolve and stand up straight, but she sneezed instead.

She sneezed so hard she stumbled. Her vision was full of sparkles too. Ruben closed the door in her face, sealing her inside the chamber. With no one to see her choices, turning around and heading toward the hearth was easy. She was simply too tired and cold to resist the comfort of the chamber.

Tomorrow she'd figure out how to return home.

HIS SISTER WAS waiting for him.

Allision smiled, excitement sparkling in her eyes. "Did ye truly find heather?"

Ruben handed over the May Day crown. Something surged through him, a sensation that made his throat tighten because it was so intense.

Everything about Sabine struck him hard. Tomorrow he'd think about it but for the moment, he was satisfied to know that Sabine was beneath the same roof he was.

"It is perfect," Allision marveled. She yawned.

"I suppose I should have waited until morning." Ruben felt a twinge of guilt but behind his sister, Arland shook his head. There was a grim look on his retainer's face. Arland lifted his hand and pointed toward the larid's chamber.

Ruben opened the door slowly. He didn't knock in case his

father was sleeping. But his father was watching the door, his eyes open.

"Is that ye, Ruben? Come…come…I have been waiting a long time for ye."

"Ruben found heather for ye, father." Allision's voice was soft and full of the hope that lived inside of the young.

His sister went rushed across the chamber floor. She believed in the power of the gift she held in her hands. She did not understand that it was her father's last request.

Ruben followed. He understood more of what was happening, but he didn't want to miss the moment. His father made an effort to lift his head. A maid emerged from the shadows to gently lift him up and stuff a pillow beneath his shoulders.

"Heather ye say?"

Ruben's father smiled. He held his hands open and Allision gently laid the wreath in them.

His father took a long time to study the wreath. He turned it slowly, examining the different blossoms. His eyes opened wider than Ruben had seen in a while.

"I think this is a crown fit for a pretty lass."

"Ye are sharp as ever, father," Ruben said. "I claimed it from the May queen."

"Claimed it?" His father looked at him, the grin on his lips turning into something from his youth. "Was she pretty?"

Ruben nodded. "Aye, that she was."

"Did ye dance with the May queen, Ruben?" Allision asked.

"I did." Ruben smiled, caught up in the memory of May Day morning.

"I want to be the May queen next year!" his sister declared.

"Ye will be no such thing, daughter."

"Why not?" Allision implored her father.

Ruben watched his father reach out to pat Allision's hand. "The May queen is a symbol of a good harvest. People need their beliefs, Allision. Ye are the laird's daughter. Yer marriage will be one that gives the Lindseys stability."

"I still do not understand why—"

"Allision, ye have forgotten that it is late into the night," Ruben interrupted his sister. "Let us leave questions for the morning."

Allision's eyes widened. "Yes, I did forget." She looked at her father. "Ruben promised to let me help him give the heather to you. I wanted to see ye smile, father."

"Ye are a fine daughter. On to bed with ye."

Allision turned and left, her steps light.

"Come and sit with me for a moment, Ruben."

His father patted the side of the bed. Ruben sat down. His father looked at him for a long moment. He pointed at the heather. "Ye faced the storm to bring this to me."

"I do nae regret it," Ruben said.

His father's lips rose into a grin. There was a glint in his eyes that made Ruben grin. Behind the wrinkles on his face, there was still the young man his father had once been.

"Now tell me about the May queen!"

MODESTY WAS SOAKED clear through to her skin. Water dripped out of her skirts to run across the floor. She was left with the decision to strip off her dress or risk ruining the dry, warm chamber. Modesty started undressing, unable to suffer the rest of the dark hours because she wouldn't remove her sodden garments.

Even though her smock was wet, stripping down to just her skin was something she couldn't quite manage. Not in so strange a place. So she moved closer to the hearth. A little sigh escaped her lips when the warmth hit her skin.

What a delight.

She turned slowly, allowing the heat from the fire to smooth the gooseflesh from her legs. As cold as she had been, her body had been drawn tight. A few more slow turns and she felt herself relaxing.

What sweet relief!

The fire was not very large and there was no additional wood to feed it with. But for the moment, it was wonderfully warm. With her soaked stockings draped over a bench, her toes warmed up at long last. She unbraided her hair to help her head warm up.

Had it really only been sunrise that she'd gone out with Temperance to greet May Day morning?

Bitterness filled her mouth. What a cruel trick of fate to see her so enamored with Ruben in the morning and kidnapped by him by the end of the day. She expected to be angry, but instead a strange pang of disappointment hit her.

Modesty snorted at her own feelings. How ridiculous was it to lament the fact that Ruben was someone she needed to loathe? She turned around, needing distraction from her emotions. They were bubbling like hot water, heating up everything inside of her.

A small candle was lit on a table.

It was just a single flame, but it flickered and danced in welcome. Modesty ventured closer to discover a meal waiting on the table. Some cheese and nuts and even two thick cakes of some sort.

Her belly rumbled long and low.

Modesty was reaching for the food before she hesitated. Really, there was nothing to debate. She was famished. With no one about, suffering her hunger for the sake of her pride was intolerable.

The cakes were made of oats. They were dry, so she reached for an earthenware pitcher. It had water in it. Modesty eagerly drank to help wash the cake down her throat and there was no complaining from her stomach over the simple fare. It was wholesome and filled her belly.

A huge yawn caught her off guard. Mere moments after finishing the meal, fatigue hit her hard. Her eyelids felt too heavy to keep up. Especially when there was a bed so close. Someone had closed the bed curtains on the far side of the bed, leaving just the side facing the hearth open to collect the heat from the fire.

Modesty made her way to the bed, sliding under the covers, and pulling them up to her head. The bed ropes creaked in welcome; the sound very pleasing indeed.

At last there was one thing in Scotland that she found to her liking.

RUBEN WAS IN her dreams.

Modesty let out a little sound of enjoyment, at last she could be free to allow her feelings loose. In her dreams, there was no one to judge her. No, there was only the way Ruben's scent seemed to draw her toward him.

It was faint at first.

She turned her head, not really sure what it was that she wanted. Her breaths were low and deep, and they drew in the scent of the man she'd ridden with for so many hours. It was more intense now because the rain and wind weren't tearing at her. Now she could draw in a deep lungful of air.

With nothing to compare with, the scent of his skin was nearly overwhelming. She knew what it was like to have her mouth water over the scent of baking apples and cinnamon, but she'd never thought that another human might affect her as intensely.

A soft tremor started vibrating along her limbs. She muttered softly and felt him reach for her from beyond the shadows, his arm slipping around her body and drawing her against him. A sound of delight escaped lips in response.

Her dream was so much better than riding on horseback with him had been. Now there was nothing between them. Just her smock and the linen of his shirt. Their legs mingled freely, the bare skin offering up another level of unforeseen intensity.

Never had she even guessed that her flesh might be capable of such levels of enjoyment.

But just like a secret garden, once she ventured through the gate there were endless delights awaiting her.

His kiss was one of those things.

Modesty felt his breath against her neck. She started to turn her face toward his, but he pushed his fingers into the unbound strands of her hair to cradle the back of her head and hold her still.

The first kiss was pressed against her neck. She shivered, never realizing how a single touch might thrill her so completely. Pleasure went rippling down her body to collect and pool in her belly. A deeper sensation began to throb there, one that made her reach for him.

His shoulders were hard and wide. Modesty pulled him toward her. She needed him closer, and she tried to meet him halfway, but he pressed her back into the bedding, capturing her gasp with his mouth.

He kissed her harder than he had May Day morning.

This kiss sent her insides twisting. All at once she needed to move, to press herself against him while pulling him harder toward her. It didn't make sense and thinking seemed impossible. She wanted to move against him, to unleash more of the pleasure that their bodies produced when they touched.

He slid his hand down her body, his fingers cupping one of her hips. He squeezed it sending a jolt of awareness through her lower body. Against her thigh, she felt the hard length of his cock. Her eyes flew open. That was no memory.

And she was not dreaming.

She stiffened. Ruben lifted his mouth from hers, blinking as he tried to decide if she was real.

"This is your bed." Modesty heard the horror in her tone, the realization hitting her violently.

Ruben cursed. The bed rocked when he rolled over onto his back and then over the edge of the bed. He moved across the floor of the chamber toward the hearth that was now dark and cold. Her dress was still there, draped over the benches. The length of his kilt was there as well, proving without a doubt that it was his chamber.

"Why. Why would you put me in your chamber?" she demanded incredulously.

Modesty fought free from the bedding. The floor was cold, but she hurried away from the bed to where her underskirt was.

Ruben muttered something beneath his breath. He drew in a stiff breath and looked back at her. "I was dreaming, Sabine."

Modesty tied a quick knot in her under dress and grabbed her over dress. "My name is Modesty."

She detested the Puritan name. But at that moment, she couldn't seem to stop herself from arguing. Her emotions were boiling.

Ruben turned to face her. There was a frank look on his face. "Ye kissed me back, Sabine."

Her cheeks felt as if they caught fire. "Is that why you brought me here? And put me straight away into your private chambers?"

Her tone was insulting, and his jaw tightened.

"Ye are in my chamber because it was the single place where I knew there would be a fire and a warm meal," Ruben declared. "The English stripped everything away in their efforts to find our baby queen. What they didn't take, they burned. Look around ye. There is naught here of any value. There is nothing left because it took every last thing we had to make sure there were roofs over the heads of the Lindseys. Thanks to the English, every last Lindsey knows this harvest will stand between them and starvation."

There was a flare of anger in his eyes that shamed her. Modesty looked around the chamber, taking in the lack of furniture and anything beyond the most basic of necessities.

"The other chambers in these towers are stripped bare," Ruben continued. "Every last bed and stool have been taken away to replace what the bloody English burned in their quest to sentence us to a slow, bitter death during the winter."

His expression was hard. In his eyes she saw the horror of what the war of Rough Wooing had inflicted upon his people. The sight gutted her.

"I am English."

Sabine's voice was soft. Her insides were twisted with the knowledge that between them lay centuries of hate.

It was insurmountable.

Uncrossable.

And it hurt more than she had ever thought an idea might.

CHAPTER EIGHT

H ER TEMPER WAS surprisingly effective when it came to keeping her warm.

By the time Modesty felt the chill of the stone floor beneath her bare feet, she'd placed some distance between herself and Ruben's chamber. In fact, she was unsure of just how to return to it.

She blushed again but this time, it was with shame because storming through someone else's home was very poor behavior, indeed. One of her stockings was hanging over her forearm while the rest of her clothing and shoes were bundled and hugged tightly against her chest. Her hair was piled on top of her head like a bird's nest, her silver knitting wires jammed through the messy bun to keep it in place.

What a sight she must be.

Disheveled...

She truly was. There was no use denying it, even if she'd managed to get out of Ruben's bed with her maidenhead intact.

Modesty looked for a bench or stool but there was none in sight. She'd made it to the bottom of the tower and was well on her way through a passageway. Here, there were workrooms. She looked inside the nearest one but there was nothing in the room.

Absolutely nothing.

"Every last bed and stool have been taken away to replace what the bloody English burned in their quest to sentence us to a slow, bitter death

during the winter."

It seemed that Ruben hadn't been exaggerating. She shivered; her stomach turned by how cruel her own people had been.

She walked to the next doorway. The chamber beyond it offered her a single stool to sit on. She went toward it, eager to sit down and get her stockings on. She secured each one with a simple leather garter before she got her boots on. Simple and sturdy, the leather covered her ankles to help banish the chill clinging to the chamber.

Like all strongholds, the thick stone walls meant it took time for the change in seasons to affect the internal temperature. The room had a simple coal box built of brick near one corner but there were only cold ashes.

Her clothing had dried during the night. She'd carried the cassock out of Ruben's chamber along with her dress. Modesty ended up putting it on because her pride wasn't going to be much help against the chill of Scotland.

Good sturdy wool clothing was the way to combat the weather.

The cassock was large but thick. The garment settled around her, granting her some warmth.

So now what?

A sense of being displaced hit her. Every day, as far back as she could recall, she awoke with a list of things to carry out before the sun set. Now, she had no idea what to do with the sunlight filtering in through the arrow slits.

The stool wasn't the only furniture in the room. A spinning wheel was there, along with baskets full of newly spun wool yarn. All of it was neatly bundled, ready for the spring markets.

Modesty saw where wax had dripped onto the floor of the chamber from a candle holder. Someone had most likely spent many months working the spinning wheel to produce so much yarn. She tested one of the little bundles with her fingertips. The spinner had been skilled, for the thread was smooth and even.

The tension inside of her suddenly eased. Wool yarn was

something she knew well. Modesty looked for a flint stone. It was near the candle. A few strikes and the wick caught. A little bubble of golden light brightened up the room. She settled down and withdrew her knitting wires from her hair and took a moment to braid it.

It was supposed to be her wedding day.

Modesty knew she should have felt remorse for not keeping her father's word, but the truth was, she was relieved to not be on her way to the church to meet Eleph Cressens.

Are you happy to be in Scotland?

Modesty ignored the question. It was easy to do with yarn and knitting wires in her hands for she needed to concentrate. She cast on the beginning loops of a man's woolen cap and began to knit.

And she forbid herself to think about how much she preferred Ruben to Eleph Cressens.

"I'M SORRY LAIR—" Eachan bit back the word "laird." His cheeks darkened before he managed to recall what he'd been saying. "None of the lads have seen the English girl. She did nae leave the stronghold or someone would have noticed her."

Ruben nodded. His father's desk was piled high with letters. He'd honestly never seen so much paper in his entire life. These were important matters, ones he needed to start dealing with. But his sense of responsibility conflicted with his desire to find Sabine.

It would have to be enough to know she was still beneath his roof.

And not at her wedding.

Ruben didn't shy away from admitting how much he enjoyed knowing Sabine wasn't getting married today. He should have felt guilty but there just didn't seem to be any room inside of him for anything except a feeling of satisfaction.

He settled down to work through some of the letters. Later

tonight, he'd have the right to claim a little time for himself.

He'd find Sabine. Of that, Ruben had no doubt.

MODESTY WAS AVOIDING thinking about how she had returned Ruben's kiss. Counting tiny loops of thread kept her mind focused while the hours passed. Knitting had fascinated her back when the two men had sheltered with them throughout the winter, for it astounded her to see a length of thread transformed into a garment with nothing more than knitting wires.

It was all in the stitches and motion of her fingers and wrists.

The cap took shape, growing out of the little bundle of yarn into a garment while she concentrated. It was a marvel really, the way just a small amount of yarn might be fashioned into something like a cap that could be sold for so much more than the yarn.

She smiled when she finished the last row. She rolled her shoulders and pushed her knitting wires back into her bun. Modesty headed off toward the kitchen to find warm water to felt and block the finished cap. Her belly rumbled because it was late into the day now, but she was satisfied with her work.

The kitchen wasn't hard to find. The scent of bread and roasting meat grew stronger after Modesty made a few turns. Ahead of her was a large passageway opening. Through it she could see two large worktables. Above them hung a huge lattice work frame. There were only a few bundles of long-dried herbs worked into the lattice now.

Modesty spied a wooden bowl sitting in the corner. It had a chunk missing from the side of it, but it was the perfect size. She picked it up and headed for the copper. The water in it was softly boiling. She scooped some up and then added some cold water. A quick test with her finger and she smiled at the temperature.

Modesty pushed the new cap into the water, holding it down

so that the wool would absorb the water. Once the cap was soaked, she tossed the water out of the open kitchen door and started to pull the cap over the bottom of the bowl. She stretched and tugged, being careful to set the hat band and brim into the proper shape. Once it dried, the cape would be very nice.

"Did someone send ye up to work in the kitchen?"

Modesty looked up to see a woman eyeing her curiously.

"I wanted to set this cap," Modesty replied.

The woman's expression changed dramatically. She blinked rapidly before she pointed at Modesty. "Are ye English? Is there an English woman in the stronghold, Morven?"

Morven was near a table overseeing several platters that were being made ready to be served. She sniffed and turned to look back at Modesty. "Not if I have anything to say about it, Aisling."

"I am sorry to have disturbed you," Modesty said.

"Sorry?" Aisling asked incredulously. "Ye could never be sorry enough for all the suffering yer kind has caused here. What makes ye think ye can come into this kitchen? I assure ye, there is nae even a crust of bread for the likes of ye."

Aisling propped her hands on her hips, standing between the worktable where the food was and Modesty. She had her nose winkled and a look on her face that was hostile.

The rest of the kitchen staff had stopped working. They were coming closer, their hatred clear on their faces.

"She will be taking supper beside me."

The staff who had been intent on Modesty jumped. They turned toward one of the arched openings. Ruben stood there.

"But…an Englishwoman?"

"I brought her here, Morven," Ruben told the first woman firmly. "She is my personal guest."

Modesty felt her cheeks heat. Ruben sent his people a final, hard look before he turned and disappeared.

The kitchen staff immediately turned to glare at her. But Modesty was too absorbed with what Ruben had said.

His personal guest?

She wasn't anything of the sort!

Her temper flared and she started off after Ruben, intent on making certain that he understood that she wasn't his.

※》》《《

"GOOD RIDDANCE," AISLING muttered when Modesty dashed through the doorway and out of sight. "I'll send her packing with a good strike of the birch if she dares to show her face here again."

Morven looked at where a long birch branch was hanging near the door. More than one of the staff members had felt its bite across their backs when Aisling was displeased with them.

"But…the laird said she was his personal guest," a young girl dared to voice her thoughts.

Aisling snorted. "Mind yer thoughts, Norrie. I will not have English anything in my kitchen and that is final. Ruben is nae the laird. If he wants an English pet, he can keep her in the barn."

"Ruben shoulders the burden of being laird," Morven argued. "We all know who made sure no one starved last winter."

"As to that bit, aye," Aisling relented. "Back to yer duties…all of ye."

The staff was quick to obey. Morven swept the kitchen to make sure no one was watching before she picked up the bowl and carried it out of the kitchen. No one witnessed the smile on her face.

※》》《《

RUBEN MOVED SWIFTLY. He had a long stride. She had to stop and listen in the passageway to decide which direction he had gone. Her heart was racing and her breath coming quickly but she heard a soft footfall. She raced down a length of corridor and just caught the edge of his kilt when he went around a corner.

"Ruben."

She doubted he'd hear her. So, she picked her feet up faster, running down the last few steps to that corner and going around it.

She ran straight into him.

Ruben had turned around in response to her call. Modesty collided with him.

"Christ, woman," Ruben declared.

His arms closed around her in surprise, but it was Modesty who discovered herself completely stunned.

She hadn't intended to end up in his embrace!

But now that she was, her mind simply went blank. Everything she'd intended to say evaporated, leaving her head swimming with conflicting feelings. It happened instantly too, like a bolt of lightning crackling across the sky.

Only the storm was brewing inside of her.

At some point during the day, she'd convinced herself that her reaction to Ruben that morning was because she'd been asleep. Dreams always were strange and distorted.

But now she was very much awake.

She flattened her hands on his chest. Intent on pushing away from him, instead her fingertips registered how hard his chest was. Her rapid breathing drew his scent into her senses again, intoxicating her just as quickly as it had before.

She seemed to transform in the blink of an eye the moment she came into contact with him.

Ruben blew out a hard breath. His eyes narrowed and she felt his arms tighten around her. A jolt of awareness shot through her in response. His strength delighted her in the deepest part of her belly.

She wanted his kiss.

It was more than a longing. Modesty raised her face because the desire was a need that was growing rapidly in strength inside of her.

Ruben met her halfway. He tilted his head to the side, so their mouths fit together while he cradled the back of her skull and held it firmly.

This kiss was hotter than the one they'd shared that morning. Wide awake, Modesty didn't miss even a tiny second of the way they reacted to one another.

Somehow, she'd never known that her body was fashioned to fit against a man so very perfectly.

No, to fit against Ruben...

Her mind instantly corrected her. Ruben released her from all the boundaries she normally never even thought about crossing. With him, she wanted to race across those lines and plunge headfirst into what had always been forbidden.

She lifted up onto her toes to press her mouth firmly against his while moving her lips. He encouraged her with a hand on the center of her back and kept her head precisely where he wanted it.

She smoothed her hands over his chest, delighting in the way pleasure shot through her. She'd never felt so good, so very delighted in her entire life. Every point of contact between them unleashed more enjoyment as if they had somehow climbed inside of a bubble and were floating through the night sky with nothing else to do except see how much more heat they might create together.

A bell started ringing nearby. It was loud and jarring.

Ruben broke off, his face nuzzled against her neck for a moment while he let out a gruff word of profanity.

Modesty was suddenly alone as Ruben broke their embrace. She leaned back on the stone wall, shivering as the chill tore into her now that Ruben wasn't pressed against her any longer to keep her warm. She curled her hands into talons, her fingernails trying to sink into the stone supporting her to keep from launching herself back into his embrace.

But that bell was ringing, and she heard doors opening. She could hear muffled voices from those answering the call of the supper bell.

Ruben had his hands gripping his wide belt. His jaw was tight but there was a light step behind them and then a girl was at the bottom of a staircase.

"Ruben," she called out happily. "I am so glad you are still here."

The girl came up beside Ruben while Modesty discovered herself eternally grateful for how few candles there were burning in the passageway. The girl looked at her, curiosity on her face.

"Sabine, this is my sister Allision," Ruben introduced the girl.

"My name is Modesty."

Allision winkled her nose. "I think Sabine is much better than Modesty."

Ruben's sister was delightfully carefree. It would seem that Ruben had shielded his sister from the hardship being suffered around her.

"Go on to the hall, Allision. We shall join ye shortly."

Allision sent Modesty a bright smile before she turned and did as she was told. Ruben was the master of the stronghold, that much was clear. The need to rebel that had sent her running after him flared back up.

"I will keep the name my father gave me," Modesty declared firmly.

Ruben raised one eyebrow. "Sabine is a far more suitable name for the lass who just returned my kiss for the second time today. Ye are not modest, and I like it well."

He liked it?

Her cheeks were definitely on fire now. Modesty discovered herself looking away because the truth of his words was just too much for her to face.

Ruben cupped the side of her face with his hand, turning her face back toward him. Their gazes fused. Something felt as if it snapped inside her. Obedience was something she was accustomed to tolerating but now, it felt impossible to endure.

"My name is Modesty." She shook off his hand and sent him a look designed to make it clear that she was going to stand her ground.

Ruben flattened his hand on the wall behind her. In a flash, he was too close to her again. Her heart started thumping hard inside of her chest.

"I will only call ye Sabine," Ruben muttered softly before he pressed a hard kiss against her mouth.

This kiss was demanding. He pressed her lips beneath his own, parting them and leaving her breathless before he lifted his head away.

Modesty shook her head. The need to deny him overshadowed any concept of being congenial.

"I need to leave here," she insisted.

Something flashed in his eyes. "I'll keep my promise to ye, Sabine. I swear it. Leave and I will follow ye."

"Why?" she demanded to know. "We barely know one another and…this draw between us is too intense."

Her voice lowered because it felt as if she was confessing and in truth, she was.

Ruben acknowledged it, pushing off the wall to stand straight. "It is intense. I've never felt anything like it."

"So it is best if I leave," Modesty forced the words out.

Ruben shook his head. "Ye saved my life. I will not allow ye to suffer for it Sabine. Honor would never permit me to leave ye back in England where I do nae trust the soldiers to not come looking for ye."

Honor.

She'd noticed before that he was a man of honor. Many men claimed to be devoted to honor but the truth was, they would abandon it when it became too taxing.

Ruben meant what he said. She saw the certainty in his eyes.

She shook her head.

A different light flickered in his eyes. A second later, Ruben scooped her up.

"Ruben," she gasped.

He didn't pay any attention to her sputtering. Ruben carried her down the passageway. Modesty heard conversation beyond the arched opening he was heading for.

"If you put me down, I will follow you," she blurted out.

Ruben stopped. "I will introduce ye as Sabine and ye will not argue further."

She wanted to resist. Ruben didn't miss it. He started forward again, intent on bending her to his will.

"I agree." She forced the words across her lips.

He lowered her to her feet. "Follow me, Sabine."

Three words had never vexed her so greatly before in her life. It was as if her temper was the tide, rushing in to fill her with a fiery need to sputter and argue. But the scent of food filled her senses, drawing a long growling sound from her belly.

Ruben grinned at her. "Come, lass, we'll resume the battle after a meal."

He wasn't going to leave the matter to chance. Ruben reached down and captured her wrist. A firm, yet unbreakable hold. He pulled her behind him into the hall and the way the Lindseys went silent made her happy to be at his back.

CHAPTER NINE

T HE KITCHEN STAFF weren't the only ones who didn't care for the English.

Sabine sat down at one of the long tables in the hall. She'd never felt so on display in her life. If there was a single person present who wasn't looking at her, she couldn't see them.

And there wasn't a smile in sight. Not one.

Men contemplated her harshly. Their eyes were narrowed while they scowled at her. The hall was the place where the retainers of the Lindsey clan had their meals. Afterward, they would clear the tables aside and sleep on the floor. There was only a single chair left empty. It was at the end of the hall, and she realized that it was reserved for the laird. Ruben took her down the length of one of the tables until he was right next to the chair.

"This is Sabine," Ruben filled the silence with his promised introduction. His voice carried throughout the quiet hall. "She is me guest."

Eyebrows rose in response. Sabine wouldn't have said that any of the hostility eased but people turned their attention to the meal.

It was a welcome reprieve.

And she was starving.

Her belly rumbled low and long. Allision looked at her. "You sound hungry. Here. Morven is a very good head of house."

A hunk of bread landed on the plate in front of Sabine. Nothing had ever smelled so good. Sabine caught the nutty scent rising from it now that the loaf was torn open. Her mouth began to water.

"We have butter too." Allision happily sat a small pottery dish near Sabine's hand. "I do enjoy butter."

Sabine started to reach for the bread, but Ruben swiped it off her plate first. He slathered it with a generous amount of butter and set it back in front of her. His action had immediate results. The men who had persisted in glaring at her lowered their gazes.

Some of the tension that had been tightening between her shoulder blades eased. More food was added to her plate. She lost interest in what people thought of her and she began to eat. The food was good and filling. The long journey caught up with her once she'd cleaned her plate. With a full belly, she yawned, ready for some rest.

"Ye must come with me to my chamber, Sabine," Allision announced.

Allision was already rising, the chair she sat in making a skidding sound on the stone floor. A young retainer shot up out of his seat and pulled the chair back.

"Go on to bed, Allision," Ruben instructed his sister. "Leave Sabine to me."

The Lindsey retainers returned their stares to Sabine.

Allision looked at her brother in confusion. "But there are no other chambers with furniture. Since we are two women, we can share my bed. It will be much nicer than a bunk in the kitchen. I cannot be selfish."

Sabine felt her cheeks heating. Everyone knew she'd spent the previous night in Ruben's chamber.

Sabine shot up out of her chair. Beneath the table, Ruben caught her wrist.

"My bed is plenty large enough for us both. I have always longed for a sister." Allision smiled sweetly, clearly still sheltered.

Behind Allision the Lindsey retainers were openly smirking but when Allision turned to head toward the passageway, those same men wiped their faces clean.

Sabine started to follow Allision.

Ruben's grip kept her near the table. She turned to look at him. That was a mistake because in his eyes was a flare of determination. It set off an answering flicker of heat inside of her. Was that wickedness?

Or wantonness?

Sabine didn't know. But she was sure that if she didn't follow Allision and separate herself from Ruben, what was flickering to life inside of her would grow until it consumed her.

Just as it had that morning...

She tugged on her wrist. The action brought her wrist above the table's edge where Ruben's grip might be seen. She heard a few snorts from the men who noticed. But Allision realized that Sabine wasn't following her. The girl turned around to see what was keeping Sabine.

Ruben released her wrist and Sabine sank into a curtsy. "Thank you for such a kind welcome."

There were a few choking sounds in response. Allision's brow furrowed. She looked around the hall, trying to decide just what she was missing. The hall went so quiet, the popping of the fire was clearly heard.

Sabine ran after Allision. If that was cowardly, so be it.

For she didn't trust herself alone with Ruben.

Laird Lindsey's chamber—

LAIRD OISIN LINDSEY had more color in his face than he had had for weeks. He held the heather garland crown in his frail hands, contemplating it intently while his captain, Arland, stood near his bed.

"So me son brought the May queen home with him?" Oisin asked.

Arland was a mature man. One who had seen his share of

conflicts. But the question seemed to make him squirm. "Aye, laird, he did."

Oisin looked at his captain. "And me son filled the girl's plate himself in the hall?"

"Her being English and all...there was a bit of tension."

"I'll bet there was!" Oisin chuckled. He coughed a few times before he fixed Arland with a hard look. "Now tell me the rest of it."

Arland sniffed. "Yer daughter recalled that there was no other bed for the lass. Young Allision insisted the English lass share her chamber."

"And my son tried to hold onto her," Oisin finished with a smirk.

Arland nodded.

"Do nae begrudge me knowing about it, Arland," Oisin said with a grin. "There are those in this stronghold who think to assure their place by bringing me tales. Ye are wise enough to earn yer place through honest labor. I know the difference."

Arland reached up to tug on the corner of his cap. Laird Lindsey had returned his attention to the May queen crown. The heather was beginning to droop now. After a time, he grinned and chuckled softly.

"It seems there are yet a few things for this old man to attend to."

Laird Lindsey chuckled once more. This time the sound grew until he was cackling. Arland discovered himself somewhat grateful to the English lass because he hadn't seen so much life in his laird in a long time.

The lass seemed to have brought springtime into the stronghold.

It was very much welcome.

RUBEN FOUND HIS chamber lacking.

He'd learned to be a simple man out of necessity. Since he'd started riding with the Lindsey retainers as a youth, he'd hardened his body, enduring the cold and rough conditions because it was his duty to safeguard the Lindseys territory.

Returning to his chamber had become a time when he recognized his blessings. A soft, warm, dry bed. Pillows and walls to shield him from the bite of the north wind. A chamber was indeed a very fine treat compared with rolling himself into his tartan on the side of the road.

Tonight, though, he looked around the chamber, feeling as if something were missing. He had a longing deep inside of him that just wouldn't let him settle into sleep.

Sabine.

He caught her scent clinging to the bedding. When he closed his eyes, he heard the soft sound of her sighs. Ruben snorted, frustrated by the way he couldn't seem to think of anything but Sabine.

She'd become his obsession. Nothing else would explain the way he'd held onto her in the hall. His frustration was nearly intolerable. For some reason, since meeting Sabine, he'd lost all sense of self control. It was maddening for he wasn't an adolescent.

Ruben punched the pillow and turned onto his side, determined to ignore the way he wanted to make an excuse to go and see Sabine. If he got her away from Allision, he'd kiss her again. That was a solid truth. So he closed his eyes and tried to sleep.

"Ye saw her face in the water, beneath the full moon. She is yer soul mate. Fail to heed the Midnight Well, and ye will live a life without love."

Norla's wrinkled face appeared in his dreams. Ruben opened his eyes, sweeping the chamber because it felt as if someone were there with him. The chamber was dark but there wasn't anything there that hadn't been there when he pinched the candle out.

Norla had just been a memory.

Her words still sent a shiver down his spine. He knew the tales of the Midnight Well. Who didn't? Long, cold winters meant people needed their tales to keep their spirits up. Peadair and Rhona and their enchantment was a story he'd heard over and over throughout his childhood. It was no different than a hundred other fireside stories.

Well, except that he had seen Sabine's face in the water of the Midnight Well.

Ruben lay on his back, looking up into the darkness above his bed. Even fully awake, he still recalled in vivid detail the way Sabine's reflection had struck him.

Like he'd never really understood what fascination was until he'd set eyes upon Sabine.

Ye cannot be smitten. Such a thing is whimsy!

His inner voice made a passionate argument, but it didn't seem to quell the desire to throw back the covers and seek out Sabine.

He wouldn't do it. Honor demanded more from him.

ALLISION'S CHAMBER WAS a fine one.

Perched on top of one of the towers, it had a beautiful view of the surrounding land. Once the window shutters were open, sunlight streamed inside along with the fresh air. There was a hint of newly turned earth and budding leaves.

Two maids arrived early in the morning to help Allision dress, but the girl frowned at the clothing they brought with them.

"Why did you bring me such a drab dress?" Allision asked.

"Yer father says ye will be going off to Hay land."

Allision's eyes widened with alarm. She looked toward Sabine. "My father made a match between me and laird Hay's son. I didn't think he would send me away so soon."

Fat tears welled up in Allision's eyes. They trickled down her cheeks while she stood still, waiting for the maids to finish dressing her. The moment the last tie was knotted, she dashed through the doorway, disappearing down the steps.

"Careful!" Sabine called after the panicking girl.

Allision stopped, looking behind her at Sabine. "Did yer father make a match for you?"

Shame nipped at Sabine. She'd failed to think of her father's plight when it came to facing the Cressen family without the bride he had promised them. Allision didn't wait for an answer. She went dashing off toward the bottom of the steps.

"Here now, young mistress."

A huge man stood at the bottom of the steps. His face was marked with wrinkles and scars, giving silent testimony to his accumulated years of wisdom.

"Arland," Allision had to pant for a moment before finishing. "Tell...tell me it isn't true. I thought father promised to allow me to finish my education before sending me away."

Arland opened his hands up in a soothing gesture. "There is no need to worry so much, mistress."

"No need?" Allision lamented. "The midwife said I must mature more before having children. I do not want to die in childbirth like my mother did!"

"Ye are not getting married just yet, daughter," Oisin answered his daughter.

Allision sucked in her breath. "Father...ye are outside yer chamber!"

Laird Lindsey was leaning heavily on a cane but he was there near the bottom of the steps.

"I am so happy to see ye on yer feet!" Allision changed emotions with the exuberance of youth.

Laird Lindsey smiled at his daughter. "I am not on me way to meet St. Peter just yet."

Allision frowned. "Do not send me away father, please."

Laird Lindsey lifted one finger to hush his daughter. "I'm sending ye over to Hay land for a bit of an introduction. Just a few weeks. Spring is a very fine time to be outside, eh? I do nae care to have ye setting off to marry a man ye have never met, so, for the next few years, I will send ye over to visit. Yer mother and I only met at the church doors. It was awkward sure enough."

Allision wasn't won over just yet. She contemplated her father from narrowed eyes. "An introduction...that is all?"

"Aye!" her father assured her. "Now come and kiss me cheek before ye leave. The horses are ready. The weather decent enough."

Allision happily complied. Laird Lindsey shared a look with Arland over his daughter's shoulder. Sabine felt a tingle go down her back for it was a serious look.

A very serious look.

"I will miss you, Sabine." Allision turned to wrap Sabine in a hug. "I hope you are here when I return."

When Allision went down the passageway, her steps were light, proving that she had faith in her father's words.

"Ye must be the May queen."

Sabine discovered that she had Laird Lindsey's full attention.

That tingle went down her back once again, this time it left goosebumps along her arms too. There was something in Laird Lindsey's eyes that warned her he had plans for her.

The problem was, she was in his stronghold, and he was the laird.

"Father." Ruben suddenly appeared. His voice filled the passageway giving away his surprise. "Ye are out of yer chamber."

Laird Lindsey grinned. He didn't turn to look at Ruben but continued to study Sabine. "Do nae make this lass think I'm halfway into my grave, Ruben." He used the cane to help him walk closer to Sabine. "I have a little life left in me."

Ruben inclined his head. "Forgive me, father."

Laird Lindsey chuckled. There was a flicker of something in his eyes before he looked at his son. "I am famished. Let us break our fast. Come, lass, I want ye to sit beside me and share a bit of the May queen luck with an old man who can surely use it, eh?"

Laird Lindsey looked at her questioningly.

"Of course," Sabine answered him.

Laird Linsey nodded approvingly. "Would ye do me a kindness, lass?"

The laird looked around, seeking Arland. The captain stepped forward in response, revealing the May crown of heather that she'd worn.

"Would ye wear yer crown, lass?" Laird Lindsey enticed her with a big smile. "I seem to have missed May morning. Having the May queen beside me will brighten people's spirits."

Sabine followed the old man happily enough. The traditions of springtime were deeply rooted in people. Her misgivings melted away with every scraping step the old laird took. If she'd somehow inspired him to get out of his bed, she'd consider it a fine service to provide.

THE LINDSEY RETAINERS were happy to see their laird in the great hall.

True smiles brightened up the meager first meal of the day. Even with the season of lent behind them, Morven only put out porridge and cream. Meal portions would be strictly monitored until the season started to yield a harvest.

No one appeared to mind. They were all absorbed with looking at the high table where their laird sat.

Laird Lindsey sat in the chair that had gone empty the night before. Morven hurried to tuck a blanket around his thin frame.

"Not today." Oisin waved her away. He laid his hand on the table, banging on it, but his frailness was evident in how soft the sound was.

The hall fell silent anyway.

"Since we have the May queen here, I hope ye will all indulge me," Laird Lindsey announced.

His men nodded with their willingness to please him. Arland was prepared, setting two mugs of cider on the table in front of his laird and her.

The Lindsey retainers pounded enthusiastically on the tabletop.

"Drink with me, lass…." Oisin lifted his mug up high. "Let us raise our mugs to coming prosperity."

Sabine didn't hesitate until she had the mug close enough to smell the strong cider. The pounding on the tabletops grew louder in anticipation of her taking a long sip from the mug. Laird Lindsey already had his lips on his own. The Lindsey retainers began to cheer them on.

Modesty might have hesitated, but Sabine tipped her cup up so that the cider flowed into her mouth.

It was sweet and spicy. Delighting her taste buds. And when she swallowed, the strong drink warmed the inside of her stomach, making her smile.

Was that wanton of her?

Perhaps but the truth was, she liked it. When she lowered the mug, it was to find Ruben watching her. Heat flowed freely through her, and she knew it wasn't just because of the cider.

No, it had a lot more to do with the way Ruben was looking at her. And the fact that she liked making his eyes fill with approval.

"Ruben…my son…drink with the May queen!"

A cheer went up, bouncing between the stone walls. The level of excitement was intoxicating, giving rise to something very precious—hope.

Hope was a magical elixir. No matter how dire the situation might be, hope made continuing on possible. Arland was passing mugs of cider down the tables for the rest of the Lindsey retainers to join in with.

Sabine stood. She lifted her mug high, waiting for Ruben to join her in the toast. Their drinking vessels clanged against one another, a little froth shooting up into the air.

"Drink...drink...DRINK!"

Sabine wasn't going to disappoint the Lindsey. She kept going until her mug was empty. She held it upside down to prove it to the retainers.

They cheered in response.

"It is going to be a fine year for the Lindseys!" Oisin declared.

His men were off their benches and on their feet. They lifted their hands into the air to cheer before they were all suddenly in a hurry to get busy with the tasks of the day. Even the weather cleared up, offering some bright sunlight that streamed in the open windows to drive the winter gloom from the hall.

"Now that, was a fine job, lass. Ye have made a fine start to the season."

Oisin reached out and laid his hand on top of her belly. "I am looking forward to what comes next."

CHAPTER TEN

T O WHAT COMES next?

A sensation shot through Sabine. It left her feeling hot and flustered and her clothing felt too tight across her breasts.

Laird Lindsey relaxed against the high back of his chair, a satisfied smile on his lips. His eyelids dropped low until he closed them completely. His chest started to rise and fall in the gentle rhythm of sleep.

What precisely came next for a May queen?

Someone tapped her on the shoulder, saving Sabine from thinking about that question. Morven stood there with a basket in her hands. She jerked her head to the side, making it clear that she wanted Sabine to follow her away from Laird Lindsey.

It was better than contemplating what came next for a May queen. She knew the answer to that question well enough!

Sabine followed Morven, hurrying to keep up with the head of house.

Ha! You are running away!

Well, she was interested in putting distance between herself and the old customs of spring. Just because she'd enjoyed a May morning dance and frivolity, that didn't mean she was going to continue on with the traditions of the druids.

Her belly wouldn't be swelling up along with the newly planted crops.

"Here."

Morven had stopped. She turned around and pushed the

basket she held toward Sabine. Deep in thought, Sabine skidded to a halt because she'd been moving so quickly.

"There's better light in here." Morven pointed into a room. "Towards the back. Open the shutters. Ye can sit on the bunk, I left ye a pallet."

"A pallet?" Sabine couldn't stop the question from slipping out.

Morven looked around to make sure they were alone before she answered. "I am the head of house here."

Morven paused, appearing to be waiting for some sort of acknowledgment. Sabine inclined her head, which earned her a slight twitch from the corner of Morven's lips.

"The cap is something that might earn enough silver to make it worth feeding ye." Morven looked down at the basket. "But ye cannot just take yarn to do with as ye please. I have to account for it, ye understand."

Sabine drew in a stiff breath. She had helped herself to the yarn. "I hope you find the cap good quality."

Morven's expression brightened with approval. "It seems to be. But the matter will only be proven if I can convince someone at the market to part with their silver for it. Until then, well, I have decided to put ye to work at my direction. What else can ye make?"

A little flicker of hope brightened inside of Sabine. Hope that she might make a place for herself, a place based upon her skills.

"Stockings. For men and ladies. I can knit silk with these silver knitting wires." Sabine withdrew the five knitting wires from her underdress. "They are my dowry."

It was a risk admitting that she had anything of value. No one would defend her if the head of house decided to claim the knitting wires in payment for the yarn she had used without permission.

Well, Ruben might defend her, but then she was beholden to him. And it was clear what Ruben's father thought she might be useful for.

Morven made a little "humph" sound. "We do nae have any silk. But our wool fiber is fine and smooth. Knit men's socks, to the knee, with a double fold over."

Morven reached through the slit on the side of her dress to pull something from her underdress pocket. She dropped an old, rotten sock on top of the yarn.

There was a challenge in the head of house's eyes, one Sabine was eager to face. She was going to prove she had more to offer than rounding with child as an omen of good luck.

"I am confident I can knit socks," Sabine stated clearly. She looked at the bundles of yarn stored in the room before selecting two.

Morven nodded. "I've a market to get to. This is not a friendly place for English blood. As ye noticed our cook Aisling loathes the sight of ye. Best ye stay where I put ye. There is bread and cheese for ye near the pallet. I will find ye after I return."

Sabine nodded. She stepped through the doorway and heard the door shut behind her. Sabine's heart fluttered a few times while she listened intently but there was no sound of a bar being slid shut to lock her into the storeroom.

She wasn't a prisoner.

She liked that idea, but she enjoyed even more the concept of earning her own way. The Cressen family had contacted her for her knitting skills, so she might use those same skills to make her own way. It was a slightly odd concept, one she struggled to accept because it was simply so foreign.

A daughter obeyed her father and then her husband. Such was the life she had always been expected to live.

Well, you are in a different land...

She was, even if the border wasn't very far away. It might as well be three times the distance considering Ruben's promise to come after her. Frustration flickered inside of her in response to that idea, but it wasn't the only emotion she felt stirring in response.

There was something else, something just as hot and oddly

pleasing.

Sabine sniffed and headed toward the back of the room. She needed to begin working to quiet her thoughts. Devoting herself to work had never come so easily to her but in the back of her mind, she knew the stirrings inside of her would be there lurking to rise at the end of the day when she tried to sleep.

And once she fell asleep, she'd have no defense against the heat Ruben ignited inside of her.

MORVEN WAS EAGER to get to the market.

Now that the temperature was warming up enough to melt the snow, merchants took to the roads to begin selling the things they had crafted during the winter months. Morven was no different.

The Lindsey head of house made her way into the village at the crossroads with bartering on her mind. The best profit would be made early, when everyone was in need after months of having no way to buy what they used up during the winter.

The village was a place where more than one clan could venture into. There were Lindsey retainers and Gorden ones as well. For the sake of commerce, both clans held their tempers, settling for dark, glowering looks.

Now that spring was here, wagons full of goods were arriving. Those traveling merchants wouldn't come to a village where there were rumors of fighting, and everyone wanted goods from the harbors. Spices, rare fruits like oranges, and other things were all worth staving off family grudges.

"We'll set up here," Morven instructed Eachan and the other Lindsey retainers.

The men were quick to put down their bundles. Eachan sat a small table down and grinned as he shrugged his shoulders to ease the ache carrying the table had left him with.

Morven began to lay out the yarn. People were already moving in her direction to see what she had to sell. They knew that when the yarn was gone, there wouldn't be any more until the next spring.

"I'll take two dozen at five silvers." A woman held up a small leather coin purse.

"Ye will get one dozen for that amount and not a bit more," Morven began to barter.

Eachan and the other retainers withdrew to allow the women to get on with selling the yarn. Morven was in her element, debating the price. Norrie kept an eye on their goods.

But Morven was waiting as well. She looked over her shoulder to make certain that the retainers were busy talking among themselves before she withdrew the cap from beneath the bundles of yarn. She'd brushed and felted it now that it was dry. She settled the bowl on the table and placed the cap on it to show it off better.

A merchant who had appeared rather bored suddenly took interest in the cap. Morven was quick to notice his interest.

"It's a fine cap, sir." Morven tried to entice him.

He ventured closer, leaning over to peer intently at the top of the cap. "Knitted?"

Morven nodded. "It is and felted. This cap will keep yer head warm for many seasons to come. Two pounds sterling firm."

"Caps such as these go for fifteen Scots silver." Arden Preyor said. "As ye well know, woman."

Morven smiled. "I will take yer offer, sir." She extended her hand for the coin.

Arden Preyor sniffed and straightened up. "Ye have no license to knit caps. Only the guild holds those rights. My guild. I forbid ye to sell that cap."

Around them, the bartering began to die down. People were turning toward them to see what Morven would say. She opened her hands up. "I am not knitting."

There was amusement around them. Arden puckered his lips,

disliking being made fun of.

"Ye are breaking the law, woman," he insisted loudly. "I will have ye flogged."

Eachan and the other Lindsey retainers stopped talking. They moved up behind Morven to lend their support, but she didn't shirk back behind them.

"The guild only controls this village," Morven stated firmly. "Not the Lindsey stronghold. There is no law against selling a cap, that is already knit."

Several men in long black half coats had come closer to listen to the exchange. They leaned in close to one another, discussing the matter. But the villagers around them were nodding in agreement.

"Aye, the laird can do what he pleases inside of his own home."

"It's clear as the nose on me face that she is not knitting."

"There is no law against selling goods in the market."

Arden Preyor made a slashing motion with his hand. "Remove it from yer table immediately. As the guild master of the knitters, I forbid its sale."

"The laird is the one who rebuilt more than half the homes in this very town after the English burned it all. How dare ye begrudge him the means to pay what it costs to maintain his responsibilities to his people?" Morven argued. "This cap is knit from our wool yarn. In the laird's own stronghold that provides all of ye protection."

The people gathered around weighed her words and whispered to one another. Morven waited, uncertain about the mood of the crowd. They might side with the guilds, for many of their husbands and sons were part of the merchant guilds.

Another man came around the first man to lay some silver coins on the table.

"What do ye think ye are doing, sir?" Arden Preyor demanded.

"I am buying the cap for fifteen pounds Scot," he answered.

"The guild charges twenty."

Morven happily scooped up the silver. The men scowled at her but with the Lindsey retainers at her back, they did no more than glower.

"This is not finished," Arden Preyor threatened her. "The guild master will be hearing of this. Even a laird must listen to the guild master."

Morven tucked the silver into her pouch without any worry appearing on her face. Her customer happily lifted the cap off the bowl before putting it onto his head and tugging it down over his ears. The gathered crowd watched intently.

"It's a fine cap," he announced happily.

"Good Lindsey wool and craftsmanship," Morven added. "No better combination."

Another man came up to the fount of the table. He reached into his jerkin to withdraw a few coins. "I'll take the next one, but I have a larger head than that bowl."

Morven happily pulled out a small length of wool yarn to measure the man's head.

The three master tradesmen looked with scowls on their faces. They turned in unison and headed back toward the guild master's hall.

>>><<<

ARDEN PREYOR OPENED his hands up wide. "Ye must deal with that Lindsey woman. Forbid her to sell any more knitted items in the market."

In front of him, three older men sat listening intently. They were the mayor, the sheriff, and the grand guild master.

Arden flattened his hands on the turned back lapels of his surcoat. It was a very, very fine wool coat. The fabric was worth a small fortune.

"The guilds must know this market will support their monopolies," Arden finished with a sniff.

The mayor looked at the sheriff.

"A monopoly is valid only within the town boundaries," the sheriff stated.

"Ye cannot allow her to sell any more caps!" Arden declared loudly. "I pay my dues! It is yer duty to protect my monopoly. If you fail to do this, she will teach others to knit. My guild will have its very foundation turned into dust. And if the laird succeeds in providing knitted goods, which guild will be next? We must destroy this seed now."

"It remains that a monopoly is only binding and legal within the confines of the town, master Preyor."

"That is preposterous! I will not stand for it!" Arden hissed. He pointed at the three men. "Ye all enjoy the money my guild delivers to ye. The laird does nay pay a percentage to any of ye."

The mayor grunted. "The laird's son had the Lindsey retainers rebuild this town after the English burned it. Retainers must be paid. It would be wrong to say the laird has nae been more than fair with us."

"But it is knitting!" Arden was working up to a fine fit of rage. "They cannot knit!"

"It would seem they have found someone who knows the skill."

Arden Preyor pressed his lips together. His face was a mask of rage, but he said no more. No, it was time for action. No one could fault a man for protecting his livelihood.

MORVEN ARRIVED BACK at the stronghold in time to see Arden Preyor standing in front of the laird. He had several men standing behind him, showing support for his complaint. Ruben was next to his father, proving the matter was serious.

"There she is!" Arden wasted no time pointing at her. "I demand that ye flog her."

The laird cleared his throat. "Morven...." Oisin couldn't finish because he started coughing. Ruben lifted his hand and gestured her forward.

Morven stopped in front of the laird and lowered herself. She kept her shoulders straight and her gaze level. No one would be finding it easy to flog her.

Arden pointed at her. "She sold a knitted cap in the market. I am the guild master of the knitters. She has no right to sell knit goods. That monopoly is mine alone."

"I agreed to hear yer case, no have my father bellowed at," Ruben warned Arden.

Arden Preyor's eyes appeared to bulge. "This is a matter of law! This woman must be made an example of! I demand it!" He waved his hands to indicate the other men. "We all demand it."

In the back of the hall, Sabine felt her belly knot. The guild masters were powerful men, and they were Scots. As an English woman, she doubted she'd fare very well against them. She looked behind her, catching sight of a door that led out to the yard.

Perhaps she should run. Ruben couldn't deny her the chance to escape a flogging, could he?

But Arland suddenly stepped between her and the doorway. The burly captain had read her intention right off her face.

There was naught left to do but wait to see what her fate would be.

"This is my home," Oisin raised his voice. "Have a care with yer words or I will have ye thrown out."

Oisin's efforts caused another coughing fit. His frail body was wreaked by it. Lindsey retainers started to edge forward, making it clear that they would be happy to comply with their laird should he order them to toss Arden into the yard.

"How dare ye bring in knitters?" Arden wasn't intimidated. "We represent the guilds. There are monopolies in place. What you are doing is lawless. How can the people feel as though their sons have a future if the guilds are not protected?"

"Now, now...I understand there is a need for guilds to be safeguarded." Oisin tried to sooth Arden.

Arden Preyor smiled, clearly believing he'd won the argument. "Have her flogged and the knitter as well. Who is this creature who has broken their oath to a knitter's guild where they learned such a skilled art? Bring forth the traitor."

The hall was silent because the Lindseys knew that keeping secrets within a guild was important. Having a unique product meant the difference between being able to sell work for good pay and worrying that the market would be full of the same product. People's lives were better with monopolies. A son might become an apprentice to a guild, and his parents could rest easy, knowing his future was secure.

Sabine was surprised to see that no one looked her way. Morven had clearly kept the cap a secret.

"Who knitted the cap, Morven?" Ruben asked directly.

His tone made it plain that the matter was a serious one.

"Sabine," Morven answered reluctantly.

Ruben's eyes narrowed. Arland stepped in front of her, offering her his wide back to hide behind.

She was grateful, even as she battled the certain knowledge that whatever Laird Lindsey decided, it would be done. And she was the foreigner.

"Did she now?" Oisin was clearly pleased.

"Sabine?" Arden Preyor was horrified. "A woman? I demand you remove two of her fingers."

Sabine sucked in her breath. Her belly knotted and perspiration broke out on her forehead.

"Here now," Morven objected. "There is no law in monopolies about gender."

"There must be," Arden insisted.

"It would not matter if there were," Ruben said. "The lass is English."

"You...you brought an English woman here?" Arden sputtered. His face was bright red with agitation.

Laird Lindsey chackled. "Aye, me son carried home the May queen. Seeing as how the English took so very much from my land, it warms me to know Ruben took something of value from the English!"

The hall remained silent for a long moment while the Lindseys decided which side to take. Arland was the first to chuckle. His men took their cue from him, adding their own amusement, until the hall was full of laughter.

"Remove two of her fingers…immediately!" Arden Preyor had the full support of his fellow guild masters. They stood shoulder to shoulder in a hard line. He pointed at the floor. "I will watch."

Arden turned to look around the hall. Sabine was certain her heart stopped between beats.

Laird Lindsey slammed his hand down on the armrest of his chair. "I will not. She's our May queen. If there is one thing the Lindseys need this season, it's for our May queen to grow. Not be cut back."

"But knitting is my guild monopoly!" Arden shouted.

"A monopoly does nae apply to this stronghold," Laird Lindsey declared. "That is all I have to say upon the matter."

Arden wasn't satisfied. He directed his attention to Ruben who firmly crossed his arms over his chest in response.

"We don't need a laird who brings home an English trollop," Arden declared. "Don't expect any members of the knitter's guild to cast a vote of confidence for ye."

The guild masters filed out of the hall, their noses in the air.

"What did he mean, Arland?" Sabine asked quietly.

The burly retainer turned to look at her. "A clan is a Tanis, lass. There will be a vote of approval before a new laird is declared. Ye have eyes in yer head. The matter will be upon us soon."

Her gaze touched upon Laird Lindsey. The fact that he was frail was impossible to miss.

"Ruben could lose his place over me?"

Sabine was sick all over again. This time it was acutely worse than when Arden had been demanding her fingers be removed.

She couldn't allow Ruben to suffer such a loss because of her. She simply couldn't stomach it. Every fiber of her being rebelled against the very idea. Which meant there was only one thing left to do.

She had to leave.

ARDEN PREYOR WASN'T a stranger to having to protect what was his.

Back in the guild workshop, he opened the ledger book. Scanning the names of apprentices, he found what he was looking for.

"Bring me Seamus, son of the Lindsey stronghold cook Aisling."

A young boy hurried off to perform the task his master had demanded. Men were working at the tables throughout the building. They kept their needles moving, but they all took notice when Seamus came back following the young boy.

"Ye called for me?" Seamus sounded as though he knew his place.

Arden Preyor fully intended to test the man. "Your mother is the cook in the Lindsey stronghold?"

Seamus nodded. "She is."

Arden Preyor leaned forward. "I want to know the name of the knitter, and if she leaves that stronghold."

Seamus nodded.

Of course he nodded. To be in a guild was the same as a clan. Obedience was absolute because being cast out meant a man would have two of his fingers struck off with a stone chisel so that he could not practice his trade. That was how a monopoly was maintained.

Arden Preyor was looking forward to teaching that lesson to the English knitter!

CHAPTER ELEVEN

S ABINE DIDN'T WANT to go.
Yet at the same time, the idea of staying filled her with dread. She was torn over what to do, but there was really only one choice.

She had to leave. The idea of destroying Ruben's future was unendurable.

Even the weather appeared to agree with her conclusion. The clouds broke up, allowing a bright moon to shine down.

The workroom Morven had shown her to was a wonderful comfort. During the day, it had been a good place to knit. At night, the pallet made the stone bunk a firm, yet comfortable bed. Inside a stronghold, a dry place to sleep was considered quite a luxury and often included as part of a servant's pay.

Morven had done fairly by her.

Sabine lamented the need to go. There was simply nothing else to do. She gathered up the cassock and headed out into the passageway once the moon had risen. A small amount of food was wrapped in a length of linen. She held onto it as she looked both ways before heading into the darkness.

"I wondered if ye'd test me."

Sabine jumped. The bundle of food dropped to the floor right at Ruben's feet. He emerged from the shadows, pausing to pick up the bundle. His eyes narrowed as the scent of fresh bread and cheese rose up to confirm that it was food inside the fabric.

"Do not argue with me, Ruben," Sabine began.

"Ye can be very sure I intend to argue, woman, and more..." Ruben growled.

He moved swiftly, covering the space between them in the time it took her to gasp. He leaned over and tossed her right over his shoulder like a bag of harvest root vegetables.

"Ruben...," Sabine protested.

He smacked her on her bottom in response. "Ye are staying here, Sabine."

She quelled the impulse to kick when he started up the narrow stairs. Both of them tumbling down in a tangle of limbs seemed a very poor idea. But it meant Ruben made short work of hauling her to his chamber at the top of the tower.

The scent was familiar...

It filled her senses, igniting something inside of her. It was instantaneous and uncontrollable. Which enraged her. But she couldn't deny that it also excited her.

The truth was, she didn't want to leave. The sparse furnishings in the chamber reminded her just why she had to go. Ruben had lost enough.

"I will not be responsible for you losing your place here," Sabine declared.

Ruben had turned around to close the chamber door. The solid sound of that door shutting made her quiver because it seemed to grant them permission to do whatever they pleased now that no one was watching.

Sabine shook her head. She was going mad. There was no other explanation for how being alone with Ruben affected her.

He reached out and flattened his hands on either side of her head.

"Ye will not shake yer head, Sabine. I have told ye that I will not allow ye to return to England where ye might be hanged for helping me defeat those soldiers."

"I cannot be responsible for you losing your family, Ruben," she persisted.

Her voice cracked. It felt as if a bubble popped inside of her, releasing all of the longing she'd refused to acknowledge since being taken away from England. "I know what it is to be separated from those you love."

Ruben let out a soft word in Gaelic. A moment later he pulled her into his embrace. She stiffened, but her body wasn't interested in resisting. He was warm and solid and everything she hadn't realized she needed desperately.

Sabine was melting, so at home against him. She was astounded that she'd never realized that she needed to be near him.

Somehow, they were both shifting. Instinct was leading the way like a minstrel. With his scent filling her senses, lifting her face so he could kiss her was more natural than drawing her next breath. The seconds that it took for their lips to connect felt like hours while she suffered her craving for him.

Ruben didn't disappoint her.

This time his kiss held an urgency in the way his mouth pressed upon hers. There was an answering passion inside of her, one that demanded she respond.

Sabine fully intended to do so.

She flattened her hands on his chest, delighting in the hard muscle she found there. Just a thin layer of fabric separated her fingertips from his bare skin, and she decided that it was a torment she needed to sweep away.

Sabine found the ties at the collar of the garment, tugging on them until they opened. She pushed her hands into the opening, a soft sound of delight coming from her when her hands at last felt their skin connect.

His kiss deepened again. Ruben gripped her nape, holding her firmly while he parted her lips for a deeper taste. It was new, undiscovered territory. Sabine followed him into it, opening her mouth so that he might tease her with a touch of his tongue.

She shivered.

Delight exploded through her.

Never had she even thought her body might be capable of

feeling such extremes. There in his embrace, she discovered an entire world of wonders hidden inside of herself.

"Sweet Christ…" Ruben's voice was raspy. "We must stop, lass."

"No," Sabine argued.

And she wasn't going to let him think about it. She rose up onto her toes so that she could press a kiss against his neck. She heard him suck in a harsh breath. It was the finest compliment she had ever received. And something else flowed through her, a sense of confidence that bolstered her courage.

She affected him just as dramatically.

So she was not alone…

Something was so very right about that thought. Something that soothed all the uncertainty bubbling away inside of her. With it gone, she gave herself fully to the flickering heat rising inside of her.

"I have no defense against ye, Sabine."

Ruben muttered the sentence like a confession. He scooped her up, cradling her against his body before crossing to the bed to lay her there. Her eyelids felt heavy because she didn't want to see. She only wanted to sink into the swirling feelings and forget everything else.

But she lifted her eyelids to see Ruben looking at her. His eyes glittered. His jaw was tight. It sent a jolt of awareness through her. She'd never felt attractive until that moment, never really understood what it meant to be desired until she saw it on his face.

She lifted her arms to him in welcome.

He came to her, his body weight more pleasing than anything she'd ever experienced. The bed was more than comfortable. It was a place full of wonder and she was excited to learn what came next.

"I want to please ye, lass," Ruben muttered against her neck.

He was stroking her. He started at her thigh, drawing his hand up over the curve of her hip, along her waist, and further still until he cupped her breast.

Pleasure went tearing through her. Sabine arched, offering her breast to his grasp. She heard him groan as his hand tightened around the soft globe. Ruben trailed a line of hot little kisses down her neck and onto the top swells of her breasts.

Her clothing was too tight.

Her skin wanted to be free, and she wanted to bare Ruben too.

Ruben seemed to sense her need. He reached down to her thigh once more, grabbing a handful of her skirt. He pulled the fabric up, offering her relief from the heat. The night air was perfect, soothing her skin.

He leaned over her, pressing her into the bedding. It was hard and yet, the proof of his strength made anticipation twist through her like some crazy shooting star cutting across a dark night sky.

"I am going to introduce ye to passion, Sabine."

Ruben's voice was thick with some promise. She reached for his shoulders, offering him her compliance by clinging to him.

He brushed her thigh once more, this time his fingers traveled over the top and along the inside where no one had ever touched her.

It was bold and she decided she liked that very much.

He pressed a hard kiss against her mouth and moved his hand so that he was cupping her mound. Shock snaked through her, but it left behind a smoldering need to see what else he intended to do.

Between the folds of her sex, there was a point of pulsing, throbbing need. Ruben seemed to know about it for his fingers delved between her folds to stroke it.

Sabine cried out. Her heart was racing, excitement building to a fevered pitch inside of her.

There was simply no way to contain everything inside herself. She felt as if she were blooming in fast motion. The colorful petals burst out while he teased that little nub with his fingers. Her hips rose up, offering him complete access. She was twisting with anticipation, everything tightening until it just gave way in a jolt of white-hot pleasure.

Every muscle she had was tight to the point of snapping. She twisted and jerked; all the while held tight in the grip of rapture. It defied comprehension, so she didn't even try to understand. There was no point. All there was room for in her mind was the way it felt to be pressed onto the bed by her lover's weight while satisfaction swept through her and pulled her down into slumber.

RUBEN PLACED A last kiss on Sabine's temple before he tore himself away from her.

His cock was hard.

It was a raw thing to think, but factorial. He'd become a man some years ago but tonight, he recognized that he still had lessons to learn.

There were more types of satisfaction than just releasing his seed.

Ruben settled down in front of the fire, very pleased with himself. Taking Sabine would have been simple. His experience would have aided him but the reaction they had to one another would have sealed the deal.

There was no honor in seduction.

He craved something deeper from Sabine. He stared at the flames in the hearth for a moment. What he wanted was something intimate. He wasn't sure he knew just how to define it either. But the need was more important to him than gaining a quick release.

Satisfaction came to him there on the floor. A sense of knowing that he'd given his very best to Sabine.

It was a fine feeling.

A very fine feeling!

SABINE SLEPT DEEPLY.

It was the best sleep she'd had in weeks, perhaps months. The bed felt perfect, cradling her, and lulling her into a sated state where she didn't have to think.

But she heard a bell toiling.

It seemed far off but persistent. Sabine frowned and blinked. A little piece of fabric fell from where it had rested across her eyes. Now that it was gone, she gasped, realizing that the sun was fully risen.

And she was still in bed.

And still a maiden...

Her mind offered up a perfect recollection of what had happened the night before. She looked around the chamber, but Ruben was gone.

That was a small mercy. Well, actually, a very large one!

Her fingers fumbled the laces on her boots while it took forever to get the footwear on. She hurried down the steps, hoping to avoid being seen coming down from the tower.

Everyone in the stronghold knew whose chamber was at the top of the tower.

The bell had been rung by the kitchen staff. Everyone was breaking their fast in the great hall. Sabine hesitated in the passageway.

Ruben would be there.

How did she face him?

Ha! Better to think about how to manage yourself!

Her cheeks warmed with a blush in response to her little inner voice. Truly, she couldn't blame Ruben. She had been a most willing participant. Demanding even.

So where did that leave her?

Was her father correct? He'd always warned her that inside of her were the seeds of wantonness because of her gender. Only strict attention to modesty would keep her from the path of lust. Had those seeds sprouted now? Was she simply doomed?

Her belly growled.

Ahead of her she could see that the benches were full of Lindsey retainers enjoying the first meal of the day. Morven was bustling around, checking pitchers and plucking a few of them up to give to Norrie who headed toward the kitchen.

Eachan was sitting with Fintan and Ardan. All three were scooping hot porridge up out of their bowls. Eachan caught sight of her and let out a whistle. He lifted his hand and gestured her forward.

Sabine jumped back.

But Eachan dropped his spoon and was on his feet in a flash of his bare thigh. He reached up to tug on the corner of his knitted bonnet. The respectful gesture stunned her, allowing the young retainer to close the distance between them.

"The laird is calling for ye, mistress Sabine," Eachan told her.

He held out his hand for her but frowned. He quickly pulled his hand away, choosing to gesture in the direction that he wanted her to go. Other retainers were looking their way, making an escape impossible.

The hall grew quiet when she entered it. Sabine couldn't quell the urge to look around. Today, there were smiles aimed at her, but they didn't put her at ease.

"There's the lass," Laird Lindsey announced. "Bring her here."

There was a spot next to the laird. Eachan guided her toward it, pulling the bench back for her.

"Fill the lass's plate." Oisin pointed with one of his gnarled fingers.

The two women who had been serving the laird suddenly leaned in on either side of Sabine to put food on the plate waiting there.

And it was very fine food too.

Sabine felt her eyes widen as she took in what was given to

her. There was cheese, bread that glistened with jam, and even a hardboiled egg. Beside her, Oisin made approving noises in the back of his throat.

"This is too fine a meal," Sabine protested.

"Eat it all," Oisin insisted.

"Father." Ruben made a soft argument from where he sat on the other side of the laird.

"Would ye prefer I send Morven up to yer chamber for the bed sheet?" Oisin asked quietly.

Sabine grabbed one of the pieces of bread and stuffed it into her mouth. She heard Laird Lindsey chuckle. He nodded in satisfaction while she chewed quickly to avoid choking. A second later, another piece of bread was placed onto her plate.

"Bring me the fabric." Oisin moved on to another topic.

Sabine concentrated on her plate. It was delicious food. Normally she would have savored it, but escaping the hall was the only thing on her mind. So she worked at cleaning her plate.

"Here...ah...yes, this is the one."

Oisin placed a small square of wool fabric on the table between them. Sabine paused, captivated by the fabric. It was a fine shade of green and looked very soft. She couldn't resist stroking its surface with the tip of her finger. Just as she'd suspected, the fabric was smooth.

"Eachan will take ye down to the tailor. They will fit a dress to ye," Laird Lindsey stated.

"But....such fine cloth. It must be for your daughter." Sabine was aghast.

"It was intended for Allision." Oisin smiled and tapped his temple. "Ye have some wits in there. Good. Too often the May queen is naught but a pretty, buxom girl with naught but chaff between her ears."

A round of chuckles rippled through the hall, proving that the Lindsey were listening.

"I couldn't accept such a gift," Sabine muttered.

"Ye shall." Laird Lindsey flattened his hand on the tabletop.

Immediately the retainers all sent Sabine looks that made it plain they expected her to bend to their laird's will. "I have made the effort to rise from me bed to celebrate the spring. I do nae care for yer drab, Puritan dress. The tailor was expecting me daughter for a fitting. Ye appear to be near to her size, so ye shall go in her place. Do nae begrudge me this season, lass."

She suddenly felt the weight of every gaze in the room on her. Sabine picked up the hard-boiled egg and bit into it to avoid answering.

Oisin nodded approvingly at her. "Ruben, I need ye in the study. We'd best go now while I have strength."

"Aye, father."

Ruben was answering his sire, but his gaze was on Sabine. While Arland helped Oisin rise from his chair, Ruben leaned in close to her.

"Thank ye for pleasing me father, Sabine."

The compliment warmed her. It melted the awkwardness that had been needling her, leaving her soaking up the appreciation shimmering in Ruben's eyes.

She liked pleasing him.

It was one of those things that family did for one another. A defining trait of a home.

Ruben's eyes narrowed. "I will see ye tonight, lass."

There was a promise in his tone, one that set off a pulse of anticipation inside of her. Ruben watched her face for a second before he turned and followed his father. It gave her a good look at his broad back and wide shoulders that only made her recall just how much she'd enjoyed being pressed against him.

Those seeds had done much more than just sprout!

"Norrie, keep an eye on the stew."

Aisling pointed at the hearth. She sent Norrie a stern look

before she grabbed a handful of her skirt and headed out into the yard. Norrie happily watched the cook leave.

"It's so nice to have some fresh air," One of the other maids remarked cheerfully.

Everyone in the kitchen laughed.

Aisling crossed the yard and went into the far tower. It was connected by an apron wall, forming a very formidable fortress. Retainers could keep watch from the top of the tower. There was a chamber up there as well, which meant there was a kitchen on the first floor.

Aisling went into what had once been the main kitchen. Now it was old, the hearth rarely used except on feast days. The younger youths who were training to be retainers used it as a bathhouse and slept there. She found the boy she was looking for.

"Ma?"

Aisling lifted her finger to place it against her lips. Her youngest son Pol snapped his teeth together instantly. She reached into her bodice, retrieving a folded letter.

"Take that down to Arden Preyor. Put it in his hand and do nae let anyone make ye stand about. It's an important matter."

Pol nodded once before he was off with a flash of his young thighs. He wore only a brown colored kilt because he hadn't earned the right to wear the colors of the clan just yet.

He would though.

Aisling was confident that all of her children would have fine places. She worked hard to ensure it. Like any mother, she would go to whatever lengths necessary to see her children live a better life than she had.

And it pleased her to know her sons would benefit from the misfortune of someone English!

THE VILLAGE WAS full of people intent on getting their errands done.

The cobblestone paths had wagons and carts clogging them, while people wove in and around with large wicker packs strapped to their backs.

Fresh new leafy greens were being brought up from the south. Dairy products and spices filled many of the carts. People were eager to pay for the wares, the sound of haggling adding to the noise of the swollen river that ran on the far side of the village.

The village was a prosperous one. Both sides of the roads had buildings that rose up two stories. The roofs on the buildings were made of solid slate. Dark clouds were gathering overhead, promising rain before much longer. People were in a hurry to finish their business before the storm broke. Eachan and Fintan were no different. The Lindsey retainers hurried Sabine through the streets.

"There it is." Eachan pointed at a sign hanging off a building.

The tailors' guild occupied two very large buildings. A sign hung near a door with a coat of arms on it.

Eachan took her inside. There were several long worktables here. Fabric was expensive and precious. Off to her right, there was a man watching two tailors who were cutting a length of fabric. He carefully picked up the scraps, placing them in a small basket.

Closer to the windows, men sat on stools and sewed. In front of them were tables that held their tools. Scissors, pins, thread, and needles. All of which was carefully organized and in plain sight of the guild master who presided over everything.

Eachan had started a conversation with one of the senior craftsmen. They spoke in Gaelic while two other men carried out a flat-bottomed basket that was covered with a piece of linen. When they pulled the covering away, Sabine saw the green fabric.

The two men began to lift the fabric out of the basket, laying it out on one of the tables. The skirt panels were sewn together, only the cartridge pleating at the waist remained to be done. The pieces of the bodice were also already prepared, the edges carefully rolled and stitched to prevent the fabric from unraveling.

It was a marvel to see. An entire dress being produced by the combined efforts of the tailors' guild. This was the modern method of production. Apprentices entered the guild at the age of six and competition was fierce for spots in a guild such as this one. Sabine took in the silver needles, pins, and scissors. To have such fine tools, the guild was very successful. She peered closer at the pieces of the dress, noting the fine, even stitching.

A pounding sound came from the guild master's desk. The man Eachan had been conversing with suddenly headed toward the raised section of floor where the guild master sat. He tugged his cap off before beginning to speak to the man who ran the guild.

To have a spot in the guild meant your entire life was lived under the direction of the guild master. Such was the way life was for everyone. To have a place meant stability. From the lowest peasants working in the fields all the way to the royals. Everyone served a master. Duty was the foundation of a good life.

So what was her place in the Lindsey stronghold?

The man came back to save Sabine from having to ponder her question.

"The guild master says for the mistress to go above stairs for measurements."

The man seemed embarrassed by the idea of Sabine removing her clothing for measurements. His cheeks were ruddy, and he looked at the floor when he pointed at the stairs.

"Aye," Eachan agreed. "That is best."

Sabine headed toward the stairs. They were narrow but she climbed them easily. There was a door at the top. She rapped on it before someone called for her to enter.

The door seemed light, but it slammed shut behind her. Someone was hurrying around, closing all of the window shutters. Sabine blinked, trying to see clearly in the dim light.

"Hello?"

She took a few steps toward the sounds she heard but didn't see anyone. She was just about to turn around when pain exploded on the back of her head. She staggered forward, reaching to cradle her head with her hands but the pain was too much to soothe away.

Blackness engulfed her.

CHAPTER TWELVE

A MAN DROPPED a length of fabric on the floor next to Sabine's crumpled body.

"Roll her up," Darren ordered his companions.

They knelt down, wrapping and rolling Sabine in the fabric. It was coarse fabric, the sort used for shrouds.

"Good. Anyone who sees her will think she's on the way to the common grave. Now get her out the other door before those Lindsey retainers come looking for her. Dump her in the river like the guild master ordered." Darren nodded with satisfaction.

One of the men was squirming. "She is nae dead."

"How long do ye think our monopoly will stand if the laird thinks to bring in tailors as well as knitters?" Darren had no compassion.

"The laird did rebuild the town. Even this building had to have a new roof," Grady argued.

"The laird has his rents. Can ye nae see that he is being greedy to bring in a knitter? And an English woman, as well." Darren crossed his arms over his chest, his mind set. "The laird is due rents. We are tradesmen. There must be balance."

The other man reached for Sabine and hefted her unconscious form over his shoulder. He headed for the stairs without argument. "The English have taken enough from me and mine. Woman or not, I will get rid of her."

He shuffled out of the door, disappearing from sight. "Get on. The guild master charged ye with safeguarding our guild. Do nae disappoint him, Grady."

Grady's lips were pressed into a hard line, but he went without further protest. Darren nodded with satisfaction before he disappeared down the steps that ended in the kitchen so that the Lindsey retainers wouldn't know he'd been above stairs.

He was relieved to know that the knitter was gone. Three of his own sons were in the knitting guild. A father had to help protect their futures.

GRADY AND RONALD hauled their burden to the very edge of the village. Above them, thunder rumbled. Rain began to pelt them. The drops were fat and frigid, proving that the season was still very new.

They tossed Sabine onto the ground near a steep embankment. The river was roaring, the current so powerful, the water was eating away at its banks to expose the earth. With the snow melting, the river was at peak strength. Getting caught in its grip could easily prove deadly.

"What are ye doing, Ronald?" Grady demanded.

Ronald had a large rock in his hand. He'd raised it up above his head when Grady demanded to know what he was about.

"What does it look like?" Ronald answered. "I am going to finish her off."

"The lass is out cold," Grady insisted. "It would be murder to hit her now. Do ye never listen when the priest talks about the deadly sins?"

"Defending me home is not a deadly sin," Ronald argued. "Arden Preyor is right. This woman will teach others and then all the men in the knitting guild will have no way to provide for their families. She is another English who come here to take what is ours. I can kill in defense of me own home. She is like a rat. A pestilence."

"She isn't a rat. This is murder." Grady lifted his foot and kicked Sabine.

Inside the cloth shroud, she gasped.

Ronald brought the rock smashing down. Sabine rolled just in time, franticly fighting to free herself from the fabric.

"Ye will nae get away from me…," Ronald promised.

Sabine looked at the river with its white water and back at Ronald. He was reaching for her, his hands large and his shoulders more than powerful enough to snap her neck.

The river it had to be.

She rolled over, leaving the fabric behind and scrambled to her feet, running headlong toward the river. Sabine turned to look over her shoulder, hoping she might be spared, but what she saw was Ronald's furious expression as he reached out for her.

She jumped.

EACHAN WAS GETTING anxious.

He paced one way and then the other, stopped to look up at the steps where Sabine had gone.

"She must have had to remove her dress," Fintan offered an explanation for how long their charge had been above stairs.

"It's been…a long time." Eachan wasn't in the mood to be placated. "The laird will have our hides if we lose the May queen."

"Aye, ye are right about that," Fintan agreed.

Eachan squared his shoulders. "I am going up there."

He took the stairs at a brisk pace. He rapped on the door at the top. "Mistress Sabine? Mistress? Are ye there lass?"

No one answered. Eachan pushed the door open, heading inside. His forehead furrowed because there was no one on the second floor. All of the work stools were empty. He ventured closer because it made no sense to him. Standing in front of one stool, Eachan clearly saw a cuff for a shirt. It was as though everyone had been sent out in a hurry.

Something beyond the window caught his attention. He could see between the building to the riverbank. Sabine was running toward the edge of the bank and then she jumped.

THE WATER WAS freezing.

Sabine gasped, fighting her way to the surface. Her head broke through after what felt like an eternity, allowing her to draw in a deep breath. But her lungs didn't want to inflate. Her entire body felt tight because of the cold.

The current was dragging her. Like a thousand hands pulling on her soaked skirts. She went tumbling down the riverbed, colliding with rocks and pieces of broken trees, before slipping around them to continue racing downstream into the next obstacle.

Pain became a constant. There was no time for the impact with a rock to fade before she was enduring another collision. Water always appeared soft, but reality was very different.

Get out of the water!

Her inner voice was correct. The only way to survive would be to get out of the river. Sabine twisted, rolling onto her back so she might see where she was going. She crossed her ankles so that she floated more smoothly.

The water still slammed her into another outcropping of rocks. But she flowed smoothly around them and plunged into a deep pool. The water was churning here, going round and round. Sabine floundered, using her arms to try to pull herself back up to the surface.

Above her the sky didn't help. There was no bright sunlight to guide her. The clouds were dark, and thunder boomed loudly. She had no more significance than a broken limb. In no time at all she'd be tossed onto the bank, just a mangled broken lifeless lump.

She wanted to live!

That desire pounded through her. It was like a battle drum, the sound stirring her need to live. She'd felt it before when the soldiers had been attacking Ruben and her. The need to take a hand in her own survival made her heart beat harder. Deep inside of her, the desire to survive flared up. The strength she'd thought she didn't have was suddenly flowing through her, enabling her to fight for her life.

She flipped over and fought against the current.

Her skirts were so heavy! She strained to reach a tree limb. The bark was rough, but she welcomed the sting. She gripped it and pulled hard. It felt as if the water tried to keep her. Sabine twisted and kicked. One foot found something hard to push off of.

She shot forward. Now she could grab more of the tree. She winced but closed her hands around the limbs, using the tree like a ladder. Her shoulders rose out of the water and then her waist. She kicked harder, straining to lift herself out of the water with her arms.

Every muscle she had was burning. But she got her hips out of the water. She rolled over, lying on the tree branch and panted. Her heart felt as if it was nearly bursting.

But you are out of the water!

She was. Victory was the sweetest reward even if exhaustion threatened to maroon her there.

No, she was not beaten!

She would not be dispatched like some rabbit. Sabine rolled over, fighting with her water-soaked skirts and started to crawl toward the bank of the river. A large collection of broken limbs and trees had collected in the bend of the river. She crawled over the jumble, making her way to the edge where thick mud presented her next obstacle.

She sat up, staring at the bog. Every muscle she had felt spent. Above her, the clouds were dark and ominous. Fat drops of frigid rain were starting to hit her, the wind making them fly nearly sideways.

She had to find the strength.

But even as she attempted to renew her determination, one of her calves cramped up. She gasped, gritting her teeth while agony held her in its grip. The pain left her panting, but she was still determined to live.

"Sabine?"

She turned her head, trying to see who was calling out to her.

Was it Grady and his companion Ronald? Were they searching for her to make sure they finished the job they'd been given?

She hugged the tree, grateful for how drab her dress was for it blended in with the bark of the tree.

"Sabine?"

CHAPTER THIRTEEN

I T WAS RUBEN Lindsey calling out to her.

Sabine had never been so relieved to see anyone in her life. The fact that it was Ruben she saw filled her with joy as well as relief. His eyes narrowed, telling her that he'd seen her.

Unlike her, he had the strength to wade through the mud. He pulled her to her feet with a soft grunt.

"Thank Christ you found me," Sabine muttered gratefully.

Ruben fixed her with a hard look. "Scotland is no place for an English woman, Sabine. Ye did nae have cause to run as though ye have nae been made reasonably welcome."

Disbelief gripped her. There was a flicker of anger in his eyes. He shook his head before he tossed her over his shoulder and carried her onto the bank. Although hauled was a much better description of the way he moved her.

"I did not run away," Sabine argued the moment she was back on her feet.

Ruben didn't believe her. He crossed his arms over his chest. "Eachan says he saw ye go into the river, Sabine."

She pointed back at the river. "Those…tailors had me wrapped in a shroud. One of them was going to use a rock to crush my skull! I only went into the river to escape being bludgeoned to death like a rabbit."

He didn't believe her.

Ruben's expression was tight and unyielding. She felt more helpless against it than she had in the grip of the river.

Her temper flared up. "I do not lie!"

Doubt flickered in his eyes. "Ye tried to leave yesterday, Sabine. I did nae ruin ye last night when I had the chance. There was no reason to risk yer life by jumping into the river."

Sabine felt her temper flaring. "I have never lied to you, Ruben."

They stared at one another for a long moment. He was huge and impossibly strong, but she refused to back down. There was a need inside of her that demanded she prove she was just as strong as he was.

"You aren't the only one who maintains their honor," she added. "Even if you think I'm a lightskirt—"

"I never called ye such a thing," he interrupted her.

"You don't need to," she cut back. "I know I encouraged you."

Ruben drew in a stiff breath. "Ye should nae have risked yer life over the matter, Sabine. I will respect yer wishes."

He still thought she'd lied. It was intolerable. Sabine shook her head, backing away from him. "I have little enough, but I have my integrity. Grady and his fellow guild member Ronald were going to crush my skull so I can't teach anyone else to knit. That is why I went into the river."

She grabbed two handfuls of her soaked skirts and lifted the fabric up so she could leave. But it seemed that even the elements were against her departure. The wind gusted straight in her face. Thunder boomed above her head so loudly, it felt as if the very ground shook.

A combination of hail and rain came with the wind. Sabine turned back around, unable to quell the urge to protect her face from nature's onslaught.

Ruben caught her wrist. "Come."

Sabine truly wanted to resist, but the wind lashed at her, chilling her to the bone.

But where might they go?

She suddenly realized wasting time arguing had been a poor

choice. The sky was nearly black above their heads. The storm was powerful. She should have been more concerned with finding shelter.

Now it was too late.

Ruben pulled her along behind him. He didn't duck his head to avoid the onslaught of the hail. No, he was suited to his environment. People in London had nothing good to say about the Scots, but Ruben and his people survived because of their strength.

It was admirable.

"Here, lass." Ruben went to go between two huge boulders. It looked as if his shoulders wouldn't fit but he turned sideways and disappeared, pulling her along behind him.

That quickly they were sheltered from the storm. Beyond the boulders, there was a cave. On one side it was open to the sky but that was off to the side, so the rain only hit the tops of the rocks. The ground was dry here and the rocks protected them from the rain.

"We'll do well enough here." Ruben released her wrist. "Best to take off that dress while I start a fire."

"A fire?" Sabine asked hopefully.

"Aye," Ruben answered without looking at her. He was surging out of his doublet. He hooked it on a stick that was near to where he was building the fire for it to dry. The fabric of his shirt was wet and translucent.

He went to a corner of the cave. He was on one knee, the sound of breaking wood hitting her ears. "With the English on our land, this is a place we keep ready."

He struck a flint. Bright sparks fell down to the place where he'd begun to build their fire. She heard it pop and crackle, light dancing on the stone walls.

The place was ancient and timeless. With the storm raging around them, a strange sense of detachment filled her.

The rest of the world and what it thought did not matter. The need she'd felt to fight for her life renewed its grip on her, filling her with a hunger for everything she had never experienced.

She'd been trapped in her drab dress too long. Ruben was right. She could never return to her father's house. Her life was here with Ruben.

She was eager to move forward into the next chapter of her life.

Without a doubt the seeds of wantonness had sprouted inside of her. Sabine tugged and pulled on the laces that bound her inside of the garment. The fire warmed the cave nicely, making it a delight to strip the wet, soiled fabric off of her.

The water had left her skin feeling soft and clean.

There were other sticks near the one Ruben had placed his doublet on. She moved over to them, putting her dress onto them. The fire warmed her legs. It dried the thin fabric of her chemise so that the bottom edge of it started to float freely again.

Ruben was watching her.

Or it felt like he was.

Her heart was thumping away inside of her chest. The next few seconds felt impossibly long while she tried to work up the nerve to turn around.

Would he be waiting for her? Or was he still thinking that she'd lied to him?

Sabine turned around. Ruben was indeed watching her, his expression guarded. She went toward him, discarding any further thinking. She lifted her hands and put them around his neck.

"Sabine…." His voice was husky.

"I want to finish what we began last evening," she whispered.

His hands settled on her hips, the hold sending a jolt of awareness through her belly. That spot that he'd rubbed the night before began to pulse with longing.

"Are ye certain, lass?"

She felt the heat from his body warming her. It was just the sort of mingling that made her feel complete. She was astonished to realize that she had never realized how alone she'd felt. She traced the corded muscles of his neck, shivering at the way their bare skin felt when it touched.

"I am."

And she wasn't interested in talking any more. Sabine rose onto her toes, eager for his kiss. Ruben met her halfway, smoothing his hands across her back and wrapping his arms around her.

She shivered in response.

He claimed her mouth in a passionate kiss But it wasn't rushed. It was needy and hungry. He kissed her long and hard while she kissed him back.

Ruben lifted his head, locking gazes with her. "I thought the old woman mad when she said I was enchanted by the well, but the truth is, I cannot quell my desire for ye, Sabine."

He opened his belt, catching the folds of his kilt with a practiced hand. He turned and spread it on the floor with a snap before he faced her once more.

"And I intend to have ye, lass."

He scooped her up, cradling her against his chest. He lowered her down, joining her on their makeshift bed.

It seemed so very natural. Not the awkward mess she'd imagined in her maiden's bed in the alcove of her parents' home.

There was harmony in the way their limbs entwined.

Obedience was the last thing on her mind, though. Sabine reached for him, stroking his shoulders and kissing him in return. When he trailed his kisses down the column of her neck, she gasped, feeling as if the flames flickering on the rocks were a reflection of the heat burning inside of her.

Need was a pulsing thing inside of her.

Like any hunger, it continued to grow, and there was no denying it. That spot at the top of her sex was throbbing intently now. Her thighs were open because she couldn't bear to close them. He stroked her again, wringing a cry from her when he touched that little bud.

"I want more than what you gave me last night." Sabine didn't recognize her own voice. It was needy and craven. She was poised on the top of some peak, desperately needing to fling herself into the void beyond.

"As do I, lass," Ruben assured her. "Ye must be ready though..."

"I am ready..."

He pressed her down, cupping the mound of her breast in one hand. A new jolt of enjoyment went spearing through her.

"Ye can be more ready...," he tempted her in a harsh whisper.

He brushed her nipple with his thumb. It drew into a hard tip, like she was cold, but she certainly wasn't shivering. Well, not from a chill anyway.

Sabine was wonderfully warm. Every bit of her skin ready to be bare. She rolled over and sat up, wrestling with her smock to pull it off.

Ruben made a soft, male sound of approval in the back of his throat before he reached up and pulled his shirt off. A bolt of lightning illuminated the cave, granting her a perfect view of his bare body.

He was magnificent.

And fearsome.

She opened her arms, inviting him back into her embrace. He pressed her back down onto the fabric of his kilt, his body weight pleasing her.

Nothing had ever felt so good or right. Her body was made to fit against his. He settled between her thighs, the tip of his cock nudging the folds of her sex.

She shifted, unable to remain still. Every touch was intense. Her passage pleading for something she wasn't entirely sure of what it was, only that she couldn't endure being denied it.

He pressed forward, filling her. It was hard and almost too much but her hips rose out of instinct. For a moment she was held in the grip of pain and then he was inside of her. Filling her and satisfying that ache that had been gnawing at her. Her bud began to pulse again, demanding motion.

Ruben knew the motion. She learned the rhythm from him,

rising and falling in a tempo that seemed to come from deep inside of her bones. It built, rushing toward a peak that she might only guess at. When they reached it, pleasure broke through her more powerfully than any she'd ever experienced.

She twisted and held tightly to her lover while the intensity of the sensation wrung her. Just as it was finishing, he thrust hard into her and stiffened. She heard him growl before his seed burst inside of her.

Another tremor responded deep inside of her belly. It left her gasping, claiming the very last of her strength. Blackness came to claim her like a cloak of satisfaction being wrapped around her. She happily surrendered to its hold, rolling with Ruben so that his back was on the floor and her head on his chest.

There truly could be perfection on earth.

RUBEN WASN'T SLEEPING.

Perhaps he might claim it was because of the fact that anyone might stumble upon them, and he was keeping watch.

But he knew that was not the truth of the matter.

Closing his eyes would be squandering the moment. He'd never felt so satisfied before. He was filled completely by the sensation. Every little breath Sabine took pleased him even more. There in the darkness, he could smile and indulge his enjoyment.

She was draped across his body. Their legs entwined and her face resting on his chest. He tucked his kilt up and around her shoulders so that the chill would not wake her.

Outside the storm was moving away from them. He knew their time was dwindling. He drew in the scent of her skin and felt his cock stir.

She'd be too tender for that.

He stroked her hair instead, slowly cradling her head. But he detected a different scent, one that made him frown.

This was metallic and something he recognized. It made his body draw tight.

Blood.

He brought his hand closer to his face. His fingertips were slightly wet. In the dim light he couldn't really see it, but he knew the scent of fresh blood.

"Grady and his fellow guild member Ronald were going to crush my skull so I couldn't teach anyone else to knit. That is why I went into the river."

Sabine's words rose from his memory. He returned his hand to the back of her head, gently digging into the strands of her hair. Sabine shifted when he found the broken skin there.

She hadn't lied to him.

Ruben felt something shift and tighten inside of him. The need to seek justice was something he'd felt before, but this was far stronger.

Grady and Ronald would be answering for their actions.

Ruben was still holding her when she woke. He was behind her, while they both lay on their sides like a pair of spoons.

Sabine could tell the storm had broken but she kept her eyes closed. She wanted to savor the moment. She'd been told to expect perfection only in the afterlife, but it certainly felt as though she was experiencing it there in Ruben's embrace.

"I do nae wish to rise either, but I fear we should."

Ruben pressed a kiss against the back of her head.

"We shall both have to be patient until the sun sets."

Ruben pulled the length of his kilt off her. He gave it a shake before he began to pleat it on the floor. The evening air was crisp, prodding Sabine into going to where her dress was. The wool was still damp in spots, but it would be warmer than her shift.

She had no idea what to say. She felt awkward but happy at the same time. There was no shame though and that surprised her.

"Do nae fret, Sabine."

Sabine looked over to find Ruben watching her.

"I am not," she muttered softly.

He tilted his head to one side, clearly doubting her. She smiled at him, and it was a sincere smile. One of his eyebrows rose before he extended his hand to her.

He'd done that at the well…

This time she placed her hand into his without hesitation. His lips twitched into a smile before he was tugging her out of the shelter. On the other side of the boulder, they could see that the weather was much better.

Ruben's horse nickered. Sabine watched as he greeted the animal with a firm stroke on the side of its muzzle. "Aye, it's time to go home."

Ruben led the animal up to the road. He turned back to look for Sabine. She took the last step as Ruben grasped her waist and lifted her up and onto the back of the horse. He swung up behind her.

"I plan to keep ye for the rest of yer days, Sabine. Best get accustomed to it, lass," Ruben warned her.

Nothing had ever pleased her more!

NORRIE CAME HURRYING out from the kitchen when they rode into the stronghold.

"The laird is calling for ye," the young maid informed Ruben. She lifted her hand and gestured them inside.

"Your father will be worried, no doubt," Sabine muttered.

"Supper is served," Norrie added incentive for them to enter the hall.

Sabine headed up the steps, but she stopped before going into the kitchen because Norrie looked at the ground. Her cheeks were pink.

Perhaps Norrie knew what Sabine and Ruben had done.

Such was impossible, of course, but Sabine found herself hesitating to enter the kitchen. Ruben clasped her hand and pulled her along beside him.

Norrie wasn't the only member of the staff acting oddly. The maids in the kitchen were hushed. They took quick glances at Ruben and Sabine before swiftly returning their attention to their work. Ruben offered her a reassuring squeeze from his hand on the way to the opening to the hall.

Conversation was hushed in the hall as well.

Sabine looked up to where the laird sat. Oisin was there with a young girl seated beside him.

"Father." Ruben stopped and tugged on the corner of his bonnet.

"My son," Oisin greeted him with a formal tone. "This is Neilina Douglas, yer bride."

CHAPTER FOURTEEN

"I THOUGHT THE Douglas contracted the girl to the Gordons." Ruben paced back and forth in front of his father's desk. Supper had been impossibly long while he waited to get behind a closed door to speak with his father.

His father chackled. "It seems I am not the feeblest between us. Old laird Gordon saw eleven on the letter and thought the girl was seventeen!"

Ruben stopped pacing for a moment. "She is far too young to wed."

"Agreed." His father grunted. "The little lass will be a good companion for yer sister."

Ruben still felt every inch of himself resisting any sort of agreement to keeping Neilina in the Lindsey stronghold. "Ye told me that match was broken father. That I was no longer bound."

"Ye bedded Sabine."

Ruben snapped his attention back to his father. Oisin was grinning from ear to ear. "Aye, ye did. I can read it off yer face, even if I did nae see the stricken way the lass appeared when she met young Neilina."

"Father, I care for Sabine. I would nae have bedded her if I were bound to another."

Oisin shook his head. "Sabine is a fine May queen. You did well to bring her here. The Lindseys needed hope."

"And Neilina?" Ruben asked. "Will ye return her to her father?"

His father narrowed his eyes. "Ye are me son, Ruben. The weight of the clan has always been upon yer shoulders."

"I know it, father."

Oisin nodded approvingly. "The Lindseys need this. This season. Sabine will provide that hope. When she conceives, we'll have a fine handfasting. Just in time for St. John's Day, I think."

"Sabine is worthy of more," Ruben argued.

"The coffers are empty, as ye well know." Oisin shook his head. "Neilina has a fine dowry. And do nae forget that the girl is a Douglas. Neilina will be yer wife when she is grown. Sabine will prove yer virility so that if Neilina does nae conceive, we shall know the cause is not with ye. A fine arrangement."

It was logical. His marriage was one that would be measured on paper, not in his heart. Ruben still bristled.

His father let out a sigh. "Such a thing matters, Ruben. I have only two children because I did not handfast when yer birth was so very hard on yer mother. She was a good woman but too narrow in the hips. Nature is nae kind. No man knows how many years he shall see. Ye must secure the Lindsey line now. It is my failing to contract ye to a bride too young for celebrating yer nuptials."

"Sabine should not pay the price with her reputation," Ruben persisted.

His father raised an eyebrow. "Did ye force the lass?"

Ruben drew himself up. "Nae not."

His father continued to eye him. "Did ye seduce her through trickery?"

Ruben shook his head.

"Well then, it seems the pair of ye should be seeking my blessing for a handfasting," his father informed him firmly. "As for Neilina, ye knew of that contract too."

"Ye told me it was broken," Ruben insisted. "I would not have touched Sabine if I thought myself contracted."

"Aye, yet the girl is here." Oisin wasn't relenting. "It is better for the Lindseys to have ye keep both lasses."

Better for the Lindseys.

That was the reality of business. Emotions had no weight. But at that moment, all Ruben wanted to do was give into his feelings for Sabine; however, that was precisely how they had landed in a situation where he needed his father's permission to handfast with her.

Ruben tugged on his cap and left the study before he argued further. He knew that impulsive actions often had consequences. But nothing had prepared him for how much more it hurt to see someone he loved to suffer for his lapse in judgment.

RUBEN HAD A bride.

Of course he had a bride.

Responsible parents made sure their children had secure futures. Being an obedient child was really in one's own best interest.

She'd strayed.

Sabine lay on the pallet in the storeroom, staring up at the stone ceiling.

She still wasn't repentant.

No, what she was, was resentful. Sabine fisted her fingers in the blanket and truly wished she might scream out her frustration.

What would be the point of having a fit?

The answer came to her while she stared at the ceiling. What she craved was Ruben's attention. She wanted him to come and tell her that there was no reason to worry. Somehow lying in his embrace had convinced her that there was no reason to even think about what would happen when their tryst ended.

How foolish she'd been.

He'd soothe her…

She felt certain of it, but that only caused the tears to trickle down the sides of her face because she knew she couldn't ask him to choose her over his duty.

How could she place such a strain upon him? How could she ask him to tarnish his honor for her sake?

Without a doubt she knew that she loved him. Astonishment held her in its grip while she searched her thoughts, trying to decide just when she'd developed such strong feelings for him.

Did it matter?

Love was one of those things that simply happened. Her mother had warned her to wait for her wedding day to meet any men because a woman's heart was fickle. Love came unexpectedly into the heart.

And now Sabine knew the truth of that warning. Ruben was solidly inside her heart. It was an incredible feeling. One she had no control over.

Just as she had no control over who Ruben was contracted to marry. He was bound by his honor to marry Neilina. That wide-eyed child who had sat at the supper table looking forlorn and so very lost. Sabine understood what it was to be away from home and on her own.

She would have to leave.

The certainty of that thought was like a dagger going straight through her heart. Tears flowed freely from her eyes, but she knew that she could not ever be the cause of Ruben faltering. She wouldn't be the one to tarnish his honor. But the only way to ensure she did not tempt him away from his duty would be to leave.

So she would. No matter how painful it was.

"IT LOOKS AS though ye are planning on leaving the stronghold," Arland muttered with more than a hint of reprimand in his tone.

Ruben nodded. "Ye might notice I've sought ye out before going."

"I did." Arland waited for Ruben to explain.

"Sabine said she went into the river to escape. I am going into the village to see what I hear over the cider and ale," Ruben said. He'd changed out of his Lindsey tartan. Putting on a drab length of wool instead.

Arland's eyes narrowed. "I'll ride with ye."

Ruben nodded. "Guild or no, I will not tolerate an attack on my woman."

Ruben knew he was saying something that could not be taken back. He watched Arland's face, waiting to see the impact of his words. The crusty captain made a sound in the back of his throat and then one side of his mouth rose into what qualified as a grin for Arland.

"She's a fine little lass," Arland muttered. "If one of those tailors treated her poorly, I want to know just who it was. We do nae need that sort of thing on Lindsey land. I'll change me kilt."

Ruben enjoyed the moment. He hadn't been certain just how Arland would react to his intention. Sabine had managed to win the captain over. Satisfaction warmed him but it was short lived. Someone had tried to kill her.

Whoever it was, Ruben intended to make sure he learned just how bad an error he had made.

"LAIRD LINDSEY WANTS to see ye."

Morven delivered the news. The head of house appeared stern. Her feathers as tight as the day Sabine had met her.

Of course. Neilina would be the mistress of the stronghold one day. The staff wouldn't want to give the girl any reason to believe they had served Sabine. The girl was young but once she grew, her mother would make sure she was taught to push anyone off of the place that was hers.

Ruben would be expected to choose his wife.

It would be best to see to departing quickly. She'd been restless throughout the night because her mind refused to accept the reality of her situation. She wanted to believe in that fable of May morning, and she had embraced it, but now it was well and truly over.

Sleeping in the storeroom was certainly proof of that. Ruben had not come for her because he understood it too. The only choice she had left was to leave with her dignity intact or make a fool of herself by pleading at Ruben's feet. It would seem that Ruben's father was planning on sending her on her way before his son might weaken.

It was for the best.

She sniffed, blinking back tears.

Sabine dressed in her somber dress. She made sure to tie her partlet beneath her arms so that the square garment covered her cleavage. The collar had several hooks and eyes used to close it up to her throat. At last, she picked up her modesty cap. She smoothed her hair back so that when she put it on, not a single strand showed.

May morning was well past. Sabine would have to fade into the past as well.

Morven was waiting in the passageway. "This way."

A chill clung to the stone walls or maybe the cold was something she noticed more since lying in Ruben's embrace. Tears filled her eyes, but she blinked them away. Her situation was pitiful enough. She wouldn't add weeping in Laird Lindsey's study to the list.

There would be plenty of long, cold nights ahead for crying.

There was a Lindsey retainer standing outside the door of the laird's study. He took Sabine in before he rapped on the door.

"Enter!"

The retainer opened the door for Sabine. Inside, Oisin sat behind a desk. There were letters and an account book there. The scent of warm wax wafted through the room from the sealing wax that was gently warming in a small brass bowl above a candle flame.

Sabine lowered herself into a curtsey.

"Rise." Oisin added a gesture with his hand to get her to stand. "Ye and I have some business to attend to, mistress."

Sabine nodded. "I shan't be any trouble. If you would send me to where my sister, Braylin is, I will be gone without any fuss."

Oisin frowned. "Yer sister is in Scotland?"

"Yes, she is wed to Dugan Hay. She is expecting her first child. I can be of use at Black Moss Tower," Sabine explained.

Laird Lindsey appeared to be thinking. "Ah, aye, Cormac Hay's bastard Dugan. I recall now. So that was yer sister Lady Alice had stolen away?"

Sabine nodded.

Laird Lindsey scoffed. "It seems it was yer fate to end up here in Scotland like yer sister."

A fate cast by the Midnight Well...

Sabine ordered herself to focus. As with all things, there was a price to pay. Today, the cost would be her broken heart. "I thank you for the hospitality you have given me."

"Ye will not be going to Black Moss Tower," Laird Lindsey declared firmly.

"You...you must see that I cannot stay here and be naught more than a mistress," Sabine stammered.

Laird Lindsey raised one of his fingers into the air. "Ye're right about that, lass."

Sabine should have been relieved to hear him agree with her, but that knot in her belly returned. She pressed her lips into a hard line, determined to do what was right.

"Ruben forbids me to return to my parents' home. I fear he will follow if I go there. So Black Moss Tower it must be," Sabine explained.

"Nasty business with those soldiers." Oisin proved he knew what had happened. "Still, I find myself rather more welcoming to ye since I know ye are willing to put yerself at me son's back in times of trouble."

"I wish the best for him," Sabine declared earnestly.

"Good." Oisin flattened his hand on the tabletop. "I plan to test ye on that, lass. Indeed I do."

It would be a test to leave. The hardest one she would ever have to face. Sabine drew in a deep breath. "I am ready to depart."

Oisin's eyes narrowed. "Did I not already tell ye that ye are to stay here? And people think I am feeble! Aw well, never mind about that. Ye are a woman in love."

Sabine felt exposed and Oisin stared straight at her.

"Ye are the May queen, lass," he offered after a bit. "It is a tradition going deep into the roots of this land. When ye were crowned with heather, ye took the arm of the Green Man on the way to yer coronation. Yer task is to drive away Old Man Winter. I expect ye to perform yer duty."

Old Man Winter and the Green Man. Fables she'd heard around a winter fire that had somehow become her reality. Oisin's eyes glittered with hope and anticipation. The English had laid waste to the Lindsey land. Leaving it stripped bare. Sabine discovered that she just didn't have the heart to argue with Oisin and destroy his hope.

Laird Lindsey smiled when she remained silent. He rubbed his hands together. "Now, as to the matter of ye being productive here. I've had an idea."

Oisin slapped the table top several times. The door opened in response. Laird Lindsey made a "come here" gesture.

"Bring them in," Oisin ordered.

Sabine turned to see a line of people walking into the study.

"Now, I know nothing about knitting. But we gathered up some people for ye to choose among," Oisin said. "Morven noticed that ye have long, slim fingers. These are the best fingers she could gather up."

The line of people looked at Sabine. Some of the younger youths were hopeful while the adults contemplated her dubiously.

"What do you wish me to do with them?" Sabine asked in

confusion.

"Ye are going to teach them to knit," Oisin informed her with a gleam in his eye.

Sabine sucked in her breath. "But...I must leave."

Laird Lindsey sent his people out of his study with another gesture. "Mistress Sabine will be out in just a wee moment. Go on down to the work rooms. Morven will show ye the place."

Oisin had his gaze on Sabine while the line of people shuffled out of the door. He waited until it closed with a solid sound.

"Ye have a valuable skill, lass. I intend for ye to pass it on."

"But the guild—" Sabine wasn't finished arguing.

"Should nae have started a fight with me over the matter!" Oisin flattened his hand on the desk again. "They will not be telling me what can happen beneath me own roof!"

Sabine opened her mouth, but words failed her. She ended up closing her jaw without uttering a sound.

Laird Lindsey grunted. "Good. Ye understand this is nae just about a few knitted caps. It's about a great deal more. The men in the village will not use murder to bring me to heel, not when the roof over their very heads was provided by my coin." He stopped and drew in a deep breath before he tapped a box that was off to his right. "I had the carpenter make these for ye."

Sabine ventured close enough to open the lid of the box. Inside were at least two dozen wooden knitting wires. She looked up in surprise. Oisin was waiting for her, his lips curved in a very satisfied smile.

"Ye will bring worth to this house." His gaze lowered to her belly. "Yer new students will be sleeping in the storeroom where ye have been knitting hence forth."

Oisin's meaning was clear.

"But the child would be born out of wedlock," Sabine muttered.

"This is Scotland, lass. I am looking forward to presiding over my son's handfasting with ye. The child will have a fine place, as will ye. And the Lindseys will have the hope they very much need. It is settled. Ye are staying."

ARDEN PREYOR SAW young Pol hovering outside the back door of the guild house. Seamus walked by and ruffled the boy's hair before young Pol took off into the street.

Arden waited impatiently for Seamus to bring him the letter. Seamus was smart, though. He returned to his work without even looking toward the high ground. Arden made sure to continue working on the large account ledger open in front of him on the head table.

Every house had spies. Just as Aisling was sending word on what was happening in the Lindsey stronghold, someone in the guild house would be willing to sell information on what Arden was doing.

The laird's son and his captain had been in the village the night before. Arden had gotten that report from several of his sources.

Now, Arden would have to be careful. The Sheriff liked the money Arden gave him but there were limits to being able to bribe the man. The knitter was English, but she was also a young lass. If the matter came to a public trial, Arden knew he risked having the bulk of the villagers turn against him.

But the letter contained ominous news.

Arden struggled to contain his anger once he read the words Aisling had sent to him.

Laird Lindsey was going to have knitting taught inside the walls of the stronghold.

Arden couldn't allow such a thing to happen. Young lass or not, he would have to find a way to destroy the threat to his monopoly on knitting.

He must!

CHAPTER FIFTEEN

K NOWING HOW TO do something, and teaching it, were vastly
different things.

The day stretched out, testing Sabine more than she'd ever
believed possible. Half of her students were gone before noon.
Her personal love for knitting wasn't shared by anyone Morven
had selected. By early afternoon, only a few students remained.

The supper bell rang, and Sabine's students used it as a method of escape. She was grateful too. There was an ache behind her
eyes.

"I promise to do better tomorrow."

Sabine jerked her head up. Neilina was still in the room. She
brought her work over, displaying it for Sabine to judge.

The beginning of the piece was quite messy but there was
improvement. "You are learning."

The girl beamed. "I am going to learn. That is a solid promise."

"You're determined," Sabine noted. She also noticed the red
marks on Neilina's hands.

The girl tilted her head to one side. "Ye must have been the
same to teach yerself in a dark corner."

"It was a very long and cold winter," Sabine muttered.
"There was naught else to do."

"I'd wager they told ye a girl couldn't learn to knit." There
was a flicker of rebellion in Neilina's eyes. "That's why they let
you watch."

Sabine felt an answering flame ignite inside herself. If that was pride, so be it. "Well, yes, they did say so."

Sabine smiled at the memory. Prideful or not, she'd truly enjoyed succeeding in learning how to manage the little loops of yarn on the thin knitting wires.

She looked up and caught Neilina looking at her with hunger flickering in her eyes. The girl nodded determinedly.

"I will be yer best student. Wait and see."

The girl performed a quick reverence before she spun around in a swirl of her skirt and ran out of the room.

Something was strange about the girl. Sabine was tempted to think about it, but the bell sounded again, warning her that if she wanted a warm supper, she'd best hurry to the hall.

⟫⟫⟪⟪

"There is no point in ye returning to the village," Arland stated. "Too many people know yer face and mine."

Ruben knew Arland was correct. He grunted, fighting the urge to curse.

"There are other ways," Arland suggested. "We'll have to rely upon others to listen for the information we need."

Ruben didn't care to leave something so important in someone else's hands. Arland reached out to squeeze his shoulder.

"I know ye have no liking for that lad."

"Sabine had a bloodied scalp," Ruben said. "I'd say she's used up her share of luck. I must find whoever is behind the attack before he makes another attempt."

"Ye are not a reckless youth, Ruben," Arland cautioned him. "We must wait for the right moment to strike."

"Aye, ye are correct," Ruben agreed, his frustration clear.

One side of Arland's mouth twitched up. Ruben raided an eyebrow in question.

"Yer father saw fit to give Sabine some students to teach her knitting skill to. I doubt it will take very long for that news to make it into the village," Arland explained.

Ruben felt his body tighten. When it came to protecting what was his, he knew very well how to manage his emotions.

And without a doubt, Sabine was his.

THE PASSAGEWAYS WERE dark.

Sabine heard the benches in the great hall skidding against the stone floor. The retainers were pushing them toward the walls so that they might spread out their kilts and sleep. She'd lingered in the hall as long as possible but now the household was settling down for the night.

She shivered. The cassock was big and wide. Sabine hugged herself to keep the fabric close to her body. But she stopped when she got to the doorway of the workroom. Laird Lindsey had warned her, but she'd forgotten about the fact that her students had been promised the workroom as their lodgings.

There was not one spare inch. The bunks were full, and the rest of the students were on the floor. Some of the youngest boys were rolled up in their kilts on the sides of the passageways.

"Sabine."

Ruben emerged from the darkness. She shuddered. Feeling as if everything was suddenly right with the world simply because he was there.

"Come." He offered her his hand.

Happiness filled her. It just bubbled up from some hidden compartment inside of her, flooding her senses, and drowning all of her logical decisions. She'd already put her hand into his before she managed to recall why she could not take his invitation.

Sabine jerked her hand back. "We must not. You have a bride."

Sabine hugged her hand tightly against her chest and shook

her head. But the person she was trying to convince was herself. "We must be stronger than lust."

"What I feel for you is much more than lust, Sabine," Ruben informed her softly. "I have ignored lust. You beckon to me like the other half of my soul. That old woman was correct. I will never be satisfied by anyone except for ye."

His words were sweeter than honey. Sweeter than anything she had ever heard.

"I will ask me father to bless our handfasting," Ruben proposed firmly.

Sabine let out a little sigh. "He has already proposed such a thing and he refused to allow me to go to my sister at Black Moss Tower."

She heard Ruben let out a sound of frustration. It was low and menacing, touching off a tremor that rippled down her spine. He closed the distance between them.

Stalking her.

"Why do ye want to leave, lass?" Ruben demanded softly once he'd flattened his hands on either side of her shoulders.

Pinning her…

Her heart started pounding. Her thoughts went scattering. Leaving her with naught but her emotions.

"Because the sight of you is something I cannot control my response to." Saying the words out loud was even more intoxicating than thinking them. "I would never be strong enough to leave if you were in front of me, Ruben."

The words came from her heart. All of her life she'd been told that confessions should come from the soul, but the most intimate ones appeared to live in her heart.

The corners of his lips twitched up. She stared at that little grin, so happy to see that he enjoyed her confession.

And then he was kissing her. Ruben tilted his head to one side so that he could press his mouth against hers. Denying him was impossible because the truth was, she loved him. He was the source of life for her and denying herself was impossible.

Sabine surrendered. To him. To herself. To the enchantment of the Midnight Well that bound them together.

Beneath the moon, there was only the magic!

STOLEN MOMENTS.

Ruben knew a great deal about cultivating his own happiness. With the English attacking year after year, he had survived by finding moments that no marauding army might touch.

Comradery with his fellow clansmen.

Finding the means to shelter those who had been burned out of their homes.

The way his sister's eyes had sparkled when he'd brought home the heather.

Seeing his father back in the great hall.

Those were the moments that he'd plucked out of a year of struggle. Hopelessness had always been lurking, walking hand in hand with the Grim Reaper, but he'd set his sights on the things that brightened his struggle.

Lying with Sabine, there in the dead of night, Ruben discovered another moment that he knew he'd treasure, long after it had passed. She had rolled to one side, allowing him to press up against her back. The scent of her hair filled his senses while one of her breasts filled one of his hands.

Their passion had been hot, and he'd enjoyed it fully. Now, he resisted the allure of sleep because it would rob him of listening to the soft sound of her breathing.

This was intimacy.

It was strange the way he knew a word and its meaning, but true understanding only came in a moment like this one when he experienced it.

Frustration needled him. Ruben felt his temper stir as well. He wasn't a man who surrendered to hopelessness and now wouldn't be the time that he started. No. Somehow, someway, he would find a way to marry Sabine. Fate had granted her to him by enchantment, so the fae folk would just have to work their magic again.

The problem was, he knew that his marriage was a reality he could not fail to face, and magic didn't flourish in the bright light of day.

Even if he knew he'd still love Sabine when the sun was shining bright.

"SABINE?"

Waking up was harder than normal. Sabine drew in a deep breath. She really tried to open her eyes, but her body wanted to just drift back into the embrace of sleep.

Ruben brushed some of her hair back from her face. His touch was something worth waking up for. She smiled and opened her eyes to discover him fully dressed.

"I enjoy seeing ye like this, lass," he muttered with a very satisfied look on his face.

"Like...this?" Sabine blinked and looked down the length of the bed to see the rumpled bedding. Bright sunlight was coming in through the open windows to illuminate her bare skin.

Every bit of her was uncovered.

She gasped and rolled over, right out of the bed. Ruben chuckled at her.

"Do nae be so flustered, lass." He offered her chemise to her.

Sabine felt a blush stinging her cheeks as she plucked the undergarment from his fingers. He didn't relinquish it though.

"Ye are beyond fair, Sabine," he muttered seriously.

"I am already fallen from grace." She tugged on the chemise, eager to cover herself. "Would you have me become vain as well?"

Ruben raised one eyebrow. He released the chemise but captured her from behind, using his long arms to hold her in place.

"Look at yerself, lass," he whispered against her ear.

Against the wall, there was a mirror. A large one with a polished surface that showed her a crisp reflection.

"Where did that come from?" Sabine was astonished to see such a costly item.

"It seems my father had a few things hidden away from me. Treasures he did not want me to sell," Ruben answered her. He eased her forward a few steps so they were closer to the polished surface of the looking glass. "This is a gift from him to us. I am beginning to like it quite a bit."

"That's...naughty," Sabine remarked.

Ruben made a sound in the back of his throat. "I believe lewd is a more fitting word."

It was...

Sabine had never seen herself nude before. Uncertainty gripped her. Was it wrong? If so, why was she so fascinated?

"Do nae look away." Ruben used his face to try and turn her head back toward the mirror. "Are we not created in the image of God?"

"Ruben!" Sabine gasped. "That is...well...it is...unseemly."

"It is also true," Ruben remarked unrepentantly. He moved one hand, stroking the curve of her hip and on upwards to one of her breasts. "Ye have such pretty pink nipples."

He brushed his thumb over the top of her nipple. It drew tight into a hard point.

"And so very responsive too." Ruben's voice had turned husky.

Sabine couldn't argue with his comment. Not only did it feel like that simple brush from his thumb had started her bud to throbbing, but she was also able to see the hardened tip.

"Tell me what ye are thinking," Ruben asked.

Her gaze locked with his in the reflection. Hunger had his jaw drawn tight but there was also need flickering in his eyes. Somehow, she hadn't ever thought about what their entwined bodies did to him.

"I am thinking…that I am not alone in feeling intoxicated by you," she answered heatedly.

He pressed forward, allowing her to feel the hard state of his cock. His chest rumbled with a chuckle that was dark and hinted at a tryst.

"How could ye doubt it?"

Ruben turned her around so he might kiss her. Hard and sweet, she opened her mouth and lifted her hands so that she might latch onto his shoulders and hold him tightly against her. The night of passion behind them seemed to have little effect on just how needy she still was for him.

She doubted she would ever be sated.

Ruben lifted his head from hers, staring down into her eyes for a long moment. One corner of his mouth twitched up, hinting at something mischievous. "I believe I owe me father my gratitude for this mirror." He looked past her to the looking glass. At the same time one of his hands slid down to her bare bottom, cupping one of the cheeks. "Ye have a very nice ass."

"Ruben!"

She spun around, only to realize he could once again see her entire bare front. Ruben cupped her breasts, toying with her nipples while the mirror gave her a perfect view of his lips thinning with hunger.

"But I like the front view very much too!"

Sabine was breathless but she suddenly laughed. It was a strange combination of emotions; one she never would have imagined. She liked it, though. Ruben was watching her, his eyebrow raised in question once again.

"I never thought to have fun…while being intimate," she confessed.

Ruben grinned broadly enough to show off his teeth. "Shall we play, lass?"

Her heart was thumping hard inside of her chest, sending her blood racing. "Um...how?"

"What every boy likes to do...I want to go riding!"

He squeezed her bottom, leaning over until she was bent along with him. Her hands came to rest on the bench.

"Will ye be my sweet mare? I confess that I want to mount ye," Ruben boldly suggested.

Something flared up inside of her. This was more than the need she'd felt in their other encounters. Now she wanted to test him just as much as he tested her. Sabine turned her head and nipped his arm.

"Don't assume I am tamed."

His arms tightened around her. "I prefer ye spirited, lass."

Did he really? The idea took off inside of her like a flame hitting dry straw. She pushed her bottom back toward him, wanting to entice him. She heard him draw in a stiff breath. But she also saw his face in the mirror. Raw hunger appeared to be etched into his expression and there was nothing she wanted more than to feed his appetite.

Their gazes locked in the mirror. Ruben's eyes narrowed before he was lifting up his kilt. Boldness was like a living thing inside of her now and she watched without blinking for a view of his cock. When it came into view, she felt her belly clenched with anticipation.

Ruben didn't make her wait. She widened her stance and felt the head of his cock prodding her entrance. She was wet and welcoming to his first thrust.

Ruben grasped her hips, sending a jolt through her. Need and hunger made a potent combination, intoxicating her. Ruben thrust into her, feeding the need consuming her.

But she wanted more. And he did too. Sabine read it off his face, fascinated by the way he looked.

As though she consumed him as much as he did to her. She wanted to concentrate on their reflection, but her passion refused to be slowed down. She felt her body tightening, the moment of climax rushing up to claim them both. She cried out and felt Ruben groan almost at the same moment. His seed burst inside of her as he held her hips in a grip that sent another ripple of satisfaction through her.

Her legs quivered and Ruben's head was on her back when Sabine could think again.

"I have never been one for spells and whimsy..." Ruben muttered against her back. "But for certain I am under the spell of the Midnight Well. Ye are me soul mate, Sabine."

He straightened up, pulling her along with him and into an embrace. He lifted her chin, locking gazes with her.

"Promise ye will be here tonight."

He needed her to say yes. Sabine felt her arguments melting beneath the need flickering in his eyes. "I will be."

Her words pleased him.

Actually, it was a pledge.

A vow...

Sabine felt the words binding her to him. He kissed her once before he released her, giving her one last look before he opened the door and left. Off to fulfill his duty to the Lindseys, she couldn't have been prouder of him.

He was a man of honor and she had given him her pledge.

The bargain was struck.

⇨⇥⇤⇦

THE GREAT HALL was full of retainers breaking their fast when Sabine made her way there. Today, conversation quieted when the men noticed her. Heads turned and she noticed the maids in the back slowing their steps so they could see what she would do.

Morven had her hands fisted into her apron. The rest of the staff shared her anxiety while they waited to see how the morning would play out. But it was young Neilina who captured Sabine's full attention.

The girl sat at the high table. Oisin was not there today,

which left the girl alone. Neilina was uncertain, her pallor pasty while she looked at Sabine with fear in her eyes.

Everyone else was watching Sabine to see what she would do.

She had given Ruben her vow. Now, it was time to lay the foundation of a happy home for the man she loved.

Sabine made sure her expression was mild. She walked down the aisle toward the raised section that the head table sat on. She stopped and touched her foot forward and then back as she bent that knee to lower herself in a formal curtsey.

And she waited for Neilina to raise her.

The hall was silent in anticipation.

"Please…join me," Neilina stammered.

"Thank you, mistress."

Sabine sat to Neilina's left. In front of her, she saw smiles of approval on the face of the Lindsey retainers. Morven nodded at her before returning to serving. But off to one side, Sabine noticed that Arland stood near the opening to the passageway. Half hidden behind the captain, Laird Lindsey lifted his hands to offer her silent applause.

Conversation resumed, the Lindseys pleased and content. It was just too bad that Sabine couldn't completely banish her doubts.

She would always love Ruben. The Midnight Well had bound them so tightly together, Sabine knew that she could never find the strength to willingly part from him.

But the world was a place of business and logic. The girl beside her would grow into a woman who would one day feel the need to secure her place.

That would be the day Sabine might be ripped from the side of the man she loved.

IT WAS WELL past sunset in the knitter's guild hall. Arden Preyor only had one candle burning on his desk. He heard the front door open and steps coming toward him. The darkness might provide a fine setting for evil deeds, but Arden wasn't concerned. The floor above him was crowded with apprentices who earned the right to sleep beneath the solid roof of the guild hall as part of their pay.

"State yer business," Arden spoke first.

The steps didn't stop. Arden looked up. It would be foolish to allow anyone too close. A dagger blade across the throat would end his life in a moment and all the apprentices of the guild would be too late to help him.

The man had a dark hood on. It was pulled up to help shadow his face, making him look like a monk from eras gone by. Arden moved his hand, placing it onto the dagger that lay on his desk. He sent the man a clear warning.

"If ye have no business, stop wasting my time," Arden growled.

"I hear ye are a man who might share a common goal with me."

Arden Preyor looked up from where he had been working on his guild account books. "I am a merchant man. Business is my trade."

"As the guild master, ye must have connections inside the Lindsey stronghold."

Arden Preyor remained silent. His visitor chuckled.

"Aye, ye are thinking ye have the high ground but ye tried and failed to eliminate the lass," he mocked.

"Ye are wasting my time," Arden Preyor sniffed. "Go back the way ye came,"

"I have a way to snatch the girl from beneath Ruben Lindsey's nose."

Arden fought to keep his expression from betraying his growing interest. "How so?"

The man shook his head. "That bit is my part of this arrangement. Yer part..." he pointed at Arden, "...is to tell me who inside that stronghold will help hide me until the moment is right. I want the girl, ye want her gone,"

"How do I know ye will not betray me and my connection to Ruben Lindsey?" Arden asked.

"Ye will have to trust me in the same way that I will have to trust the name ye give me," the man said. "I will expect ye to give me the right code word to prove to yer connection that they are to assist me."

His unnamed visitor was no fool. Subterfuge required code-words and phrases so that the participants could avoid being discovered.

The man stepped forward. The meager light from the candle washed over him, illuminating the kilt he wore.

Gordon colors.

"I am Gareth Gordon. I am going to steal Ruben's woman."

Arden Preyor smiled. His lips split wide to show his teeth. He reached into the neck of his shirt, pulling on a worn length of leather cord. A ring came into view. He reached over and poured some sealing wax onto a little square of paper and pressed the face of the ring into it.

"Find Aisling, the cook. Give her this."

Gareth grinned. He took the paper, tucking it into his doublet. Perhaps Arden should have felt guilty for the look on Gareth's face was menacing. But Arden was too focused on regaining his exclusivity in the market.

It was a necessary thing, ridding his environment of any competition.

CHAPTER SIXTEEN

T HE BELLS BEGAN to ring long after supper had finished.
Ruben stiffened. "I must go."

He rolled away from Sabine, leaving the bed a second later.
He jerked his shirt on and belted his kilt into place quickly before
he headed out of the chamber.

So that was why he always pleated up the fabric of his kilt
before going to sleep.

Sabine wasn't happy to discover the meaning behind Ruben's
habits. For tonight, she was being reminded that the land they
resided on was under threat of attack.

She already felt every moment they had together was precious. Now, there was a chill gripping her heart. She tried not to
think that she might have just spent her last intimate moments
with Ruben but worry crept past her good intentions.

The bells continued to ring, summoning every able-bodied
man to the defense of the stronghold. Sabine hurried through
dressing so she might see what the threat was.

When she made it to the ground floor, the illuminated hall
was full of men. She made it to the passageway opening, stooping
down to see between the maids who were clustered around the
opening. The men standing in front of Ruben wore kilts. Sabine
had only a moment of relief before she recognized the colors of
those kilts.

They were Hay colors. A shiver went down her back. The
last time she'd seen those colors had been when her sister was

abducted.

"I have called ye friend for a long time, Ruben."

Ruben stood in the hall, facing off with the man. "There is no reason for ye to be angry, Dugan."

"No cause?" Dugan Hay demanded. "I trusted ye with a letter for Braylin's sister, Modesty. Now, I hear ye took her away. It was my doing sending ye down to the Hawlyn home. I cannot turn a blind eye to you taking my wife's sister."

"Some soldiers attacked Modesty. I had to take her with me else she might have faced English justice," Ruben declared. "Sabine and I are going to be handfasted."

A sound of agreement rippled through the retainers clustered tightly around Dugan and Ruben.

"Handfasted?" Dugan shook his head. "Braylin and Modesty are Puritans. They do nae consider a handfasting respectful. Give the girl to me. I will take her back to Black Moss Tower."

Ruben appeared unwilling to answer. The tension in the hall tightened. Without a doubt, the two men were edging closer to violence.

"Let me through." Sabine started forward, determined to prevent Ruben from fighting.

"Nae not."

It was Aisling who refused Sabine.

The cook turned around, blocking out Sabine's view. But she heard Dugan let out a clipped word of profanity. A moment later the sounds of a scuffle rose from the hall.

Sabine had her own scuffle to contend with.

Several maids turned around and started pushing her away from the hall. Sabine wanted to resist but there were too many of them. Her feet just slid backwards across the worn stone floor.

"Bring her here," Aisling instructed her clanswomen.

The group half carried Sabine into the kitchen and then further on to the still room.

"Ye will be staying right here, mistress Hawlyn," Aisling declared. "The men will sort matters out between them. It is no place for women."

"I can stop them," Sabine said.

"Men fight," Aisling offered in a knowing tone. "Best for ye to stay out of it. No man wants a woman talking for him while his men are watching."

"But they are fighting because of me," Sabine argued.

"The cause is irrelevant," Aisling insisted. "The Hay need to know that our next laird is a good fighter. That the Lindseys are strong. If we allow Dugan Hay to take ye away, the tale will spread far and wide. Others will come here thinking to take what we have. Weakness has a stench that attracts predators."

There was a murmur of agreement among those watching. But the sounds of furniture crashing from the hall drew their attention.

The maids wanted to get back to the hall. Aisling waved them on. They were quick to take advantage of the cook's permission, scurrying through the doorway, across the kitchen, and back into the passageway.

"Stay here, mistress. If I have to bring ye back, I shall bar the door." Aisling issued her warning with a stern look while she fingered the keys attached to her belt. The little jingle of those keys was enough to make Sabine nod.

The cook turned and disappeared while the sound of the fight continued. Sabine took a few steps but then turned around and paced back in the opposite direction because the door of the still room did, in fact, have a latch with a lock hanging from it.

Would Ruben resent her if she tried to break up the fight?

She was rooted in place while she contemplated that idea. It wasn't the first time Ruben had fought over her, either. He'd fought with Jasper Hardwin on May Day morning.

Was Aisling right to tell her to leave it be?

The cook certainly knew Ruben better than Sabine possibly could.

There was another crash from the hall. Sabine whirled around and lost the battle to stay where Aisling had put her. She hurried out into the dark passageway, intent on breaking up the fight. Her sister would certainly agree.

Someone grabbed a handful of her dress, dragging her backward.

"Well now, mistress, do nae ye worry about Ruben…I will be letting him know just where to find ye if he wants to rescue ye." The man holding her chuckled. It was by far the most distorted, evil sound she'd ever heard, filling her with icy dread.

"Aye, ye are fine bait," he muttered before he released her. Sabine had a single moment of standing free before pain exploded on the back of her head once more. She actually noticed the rush of blackness coming for her like a wave washing up onto shore. It hit her full in the face, buckling her knees and dragging her into oblivion.

⋙⋘

"ENOUGH." IT WAS Arland who spoke. "Pull them apart."

The Lindsey retainers reluctantly stopped cheering. They dived in to break up the fight at their captain's demand. Ruben glared at the veteran captain opening his mouth to argue.

"Yer father will hear at some point." Arland crossed his arms over his chest and stared straight at Ruben.

Ruben narrowed his eyes, but he used his shirtsleeve to wipe his forehead and didn't resume the scuffle. He and Dugan stared at one another for a long, awkward moment while they panted.

"Have some cider and discuss the matter," Arland suggested.

"There is naught to discuss," Ruben insisted.

"There most assuredly is," Dugan declared.

Ruben turned to glare at Dugan Hay.

"I am nae returning to me wife to tell her that it is true. Ye took her sister," Dugan cut back. He pointed at Ruben.

"Ye do nae know the circumstances, Dugan. I could not leave that lass there to face possible retribution," Ruben said.

Dugan paused a moment to consider what Ruben had said. But he shook his head. "Sabine can be naught but a mistress in yer house. I am bastard born, Ruben. That is a life that is hard to live."

Ruben bit back the argument he wanted to make. Instead, he drew in a breath and let it out before responding. "I will handfast with Sabine. Ye can witness the ceremony and the contracts. Sabine has agreed."

Dugan took a moment to think over what Ruben was offering. "Ye will add a promise to the lass that she is free to leave here and come to Black Moss Tower."

Ruben's expression tightened. Dugan didn't relent. He shot his friend an unrelenting look. "I had a stepmother, Ruben. She went so far as to have me wife torn from her family in a quest to make sure my future was ruined. I have me father to stand on my side, but yer father is old. If something happens to ye, there must be a place secured for Sabine. That place is Black Moss Tower."

Ruben didn't like the suggestion. No one in the hall missed the tight set of his jaw. But he nodded, recognizing it was a logical solution.

"Bring some cider," Arland issued the command.

There was a shuffle in the opening to the passageway. Norrie turned to go see to the chore when two of the older maids pointed her toward the kitchen. The retainers, both Lindsey and Hay, began to right the benches, restoring order to the hall.

Norrie screamed.

The sound gained instant response. Ruben rushed into the passageway along with most of the retainers. Norrie turned her wide eyes toward him. Lying on the stone floor was Aisling. A puddle of blood seeping out from her body.

A sheet of parchment was placed on top of the cook's body. A single lock of hair on it.

It was Sabine's.

Without a doubt Ruben knew the hair belonged to Sabine. What made his mouth go dry was the fact that Aisling was dead to prove that whoever had taken Sabine was very serious. He picked up the parchment to read the message.

"If ye want yer woman, meet me within the hour at the mill. Just you or I swear yer woman will be dead like yer cook before ye can do anything to help her. Gareth Gorden."

SOMEONE THREW WATER on her.

Sabine sputtered, waking up with a jolt. The water was frigid. It soaked into her clothing allowing the wind to chill her further. Her instinct was to huddle but her arms were tied.

"I will be insisting that ye stay right there, mistress."

Sabine recalled that voice. He'd called her bait. Her arms were secured behind her, some cord biting into the skin of her wrists. She pulled against the binding, but the pain became too intense.

Gareth was amused by her struggle. Or her pain. Perhaps both. The sound of his amusement made her shudder.

He struck a flint. In the blackness surrounding her, suddenly there was light.

"I hope ye find yerself very securely bound, mistress," Gareth continued. There was a hint of true amusement in his tone that sent a chill down her back.

This was a man who enjoyed toying with those less fortunate.

He held a candle over the small fire he'd started in a bowl of tinder. It caught, offering her relief from the darkness but she decided she wasn't relieved to see what the darkness had hidden from her.

Gareth had bound her to a beam holding up the second floor of the woolworks building. Around her there were fresh fleece pelts. Only a few for the spring were new but even so, her eyes widened in alarm.

"Ye see yer circumstances…do ye nae?" Gareth moved the candle back and forth in front of her face.

Flames were strictly forbidden in the wool works building. A few pelts were stored near the walls but there were little tuffs of wool on the floor. On one side, a pile was sitting next to a broom, but the nature of wool was that the fibers scattered easily. Hence the rule of no open flames.

A fire here would spread quickly.

She pulled again on her bindings.

"I hear ye are a Puritan." Gareth mocked her efforts to free herself. "And that yer father refused to recant now that the English queen demands a return to the Roman Church."

Gareth sat the candle in a simple pottery stand in front of her. He looked over at a pelt and smiled grotesquely at her.

"Tell me, would yer father be pleased to hear ye went to the stake rather than lived in dishonor?"

Sabine shook her head.

"Are ye sure?" Gareth continued. "I doubt he'd enjoy knowing ye have played the slut to a Scotsman."

He moved off toward the wall. He hooked one of the pelts, pulling it over to lay it against her legs.

"However, the opinion that matters is Ruben Lindsey's."

Gareth placed a second and third pelt around her. She looked at the distance between herself and the candle.

"Do nae worry. This candle is nae for ye."

Gareth walked toward her. Slowly. Giving her time to shiver in dread before he covered the last few paces.

"If ye were nae Ruben's, I'd enjoy using ye." Gareth spit on the floor, disgust drawing his lips thin. "I won't be reduced to tasting his leavings."

"What are you going to do with me?" Perhaps it might have been wiser to remain silent. Sabine couldn't seem to duck her chin and be meek.

Gareth smiled at her. "Ye have some spirit. Hmmm." He leaned close, looking down at her cleavage. Sabine jerked on her bindings.

"As I said. I will not lower myself to Ruben's leavings."

Gareth walked behind her, tugging on the leather binding her. He grunted approval before he leaned down next to her ear and whispered.

"My archer is waiting for the signal on just where to aim his fire arrow. Yer lover will have a choice. He can save ye or keep the dowry from the Douglases. I know what I'd choose."

"Dowry?" Sabine couldn't help but ask. "But why did you give up Neilina if you wanted to keep the dowry?"

Gareth walked around her to the candle. "Business is done between men. Women are practically useless. Now that Ruben has had ye, the only thing ye are good for is being bait. He might decide to let ye burn."

Gareth pinched out the candle, casting her back into darkness. She heard him cross the floor. There was a scratching sound and then one of the window shutters was opened. Sabine blinked, trying to restore her night vision so that the starlight would be enough for her to see with.

But it would take time.

Gareth opened the other shutter and left. She heard his steps receding before they were gone altogether.

Time tormented her. Every breath she drew might be her last.

No.

She wasn't willing to wait for her fate. There was so much of life left to live. She'd been a fool to worry about what might happen in the future. Life was lived in the moment. Even if she'd married Eleph Cressens, there was no certainty of her future being free of calamity.

She had love. It was a beautiful, wonderful gift. Gareth Gordon wouldn't destroy it. Not while she still drew breath.

Sabine sealed herself against the pain of the bindings before she began to rub the cords against the beam she was bound to.

She was much more than bait.

She had to be!

CHAPTER SEVENTEEN

T HE MILL WASN'T too far from the Lindsey stronghold. Set on the edge of the river, a large grinding stone was housed in its main room. Gareth Gordon was waiting for Ruben on the upper floor. He had the twin halves of the shutters open, a candle illuminating his face as though he was sitting comfortably in his own stronghold.

"Truthfully, I had wondered if ye might be glad to be rid of the girl," Gareth said when he spied Ruben. "There are other tarts to enjoy."

Rueben bristled at the insult given so casually to Sabine. Arguing over labels wouldn't help him save her, though.

"There is a place for ye in hell," Ruben stated.

Gareth grinned in response to the threat. "Because I killed yer cook?"

Ruben nodded. "That's one reason."

"Ah, she was a traitor," Gareth chuckled. "Allowed me into yer stronghold under the cover of night. She should be grateful I gave her a quick death. On Gordon land, traitors are dealt with harshly."

"What do ye want, Gareth?" Ruben remained focused. "Traitor or no, killing a woman beneath me roof is nae forgivable."

Gareth stretched his arms out wide. "Do I sound as though I am asking ye for forgiveness?" He spit on the floor.

"Where is Sabine?"

Gareth's lips curled up into a grin. He pointed out the open shutters. "I left yer doxy over in the workhouse. Tied her up good and tight. Even tucked several fresh fleece pelts around her legs. My archer is waiting with a fire arrow. I suggest ye do nae kill me or ye will watch yer woman burn."

Dread filled him. He hoped it wasn't true.

Ruben looked across to the workhouse. The sky was mostly clear tonight. Even if the moon was only a crescent, there was ample starlight. It illuminated the open shutters, showing him a figure just inside the window.

His blood ran cold. He couldn't give up Neilina. There was no way he could reconcile himself to handing over a child to a monster such as Gareth Gordon.

But Sabine would pay the price if he didn't.

He'd have to kill Gareth before he gave any commands.

Ruben felt his body tense. His eyes narrowed.

"Killing me is a bad idea." Gareth read Ruben's body language. "I have two witnesses in the dark here. Both in different corners of the room. Ye can nae kill them both before one of them signals the archer."

"State yer demands," Ruben growled.

Gareth pulled something from his doublet. The parchment crackled when he unfolded it.

"I want the dowry from the Douglases."

Ruben frowned. He looked at the parchment.

"The Douglases placed it with the bankers for safe keeping," Gareth said. "They will nae release it in spite of the fact that I have a priest to swear that the wedding was performed and consummated."

Gareth dropped a small pottery ink well on the stool in front of him. "Sign it and ye can go save yer doxy while I ride away."

Ruben crossed his arms over his chest. The quill remained in the air between him and Gareth.

"Who is Neilina?" Ruben asked pointedly.

"She is my wife; I stole her on her way to you," Gareth responded. He had lost some of his swagger while Ruben hesitated.

"But those bankers see only the contracts."

"And the girl who arrived in me stronghold?" Ruben asked.

Gareth snorted. "Now that was a fine bit of trickery. Ye must admit it was clever. Too bad the lass was nae old enough for ye to wed. Some things cannot be undone after all."

"Things such as wedding contracts," Ruben remarked dryly.

Gareth sobered. "I took Neilina Douglas and made her my wife. But ye are correct. If I fight ye in a court of law, I'll lose part of the dowry." He grinned again. "So I took yer woman too."

Gareth was pleased with himself. He'd clearly judged Ruben to be a man who would let his heart lead the way.

Ruben admitted that he was precisely that when it came to Sabine. The man was cruel. The sort who enjoyed inflicting pain upon others. One bad move and Sabine would pay with her life.

Ruben took the quill. Gareth watched intently. Dipping the end of the quill into the ink was a risk. Gareth might not keep his word. But it was the only chance Sabine had. So he signed the parchment. The ink glistened in the candlelight until it soaked into the paper.

Gareth folded it and tucked it back into his doublet. He sent Ruben a very satisfied smile.

"Better run Lindsey."

Ruben turned to see twin points of light appear below him in the yard. They rose up and then flew through the night toward the workhouse. One hit the back of the workhouse and the other the front. The arrow in the front easily caught the dry thatch on the roof of the building. The flames grew, illuminating Sabine where she struggled to free herself.

He swung out of the window, dropped on the ground while Gareth laughed behind him.

SABINE GASPED WHEN the arrow hit the window frame in front of her. Thatch was very good at keeping water out of buildings, but it was also very flammable. The single point of flame easily caught and spread.

The smoke blew toward her face and overwhelmed her senses. It carried cinders that stung her cheeks. She looked down at the fleece gathered around her legs.

She needed to keep fighting!

She pulled on her binds again, rubbing it faster against the beam. She had countless splinters in her wrists now, the skin torn and painful. The cords still held.

The scent of smoke grew stronger.

The heat was increasing enough to become hot on her face.

She jerked her hands up and shoved them down hard. There was a snap. She pitched forward, stumbling when the cord broke at long last.

"Run, Lindsey!"

Sabine looked through the flames at the yard below. Gareth's taunting voice came with the wind. She saw Ruben running but she also saw an archer taking aim at his back.

"Archer!" Sabine yelled.

Ruben jerked around. He dropped to the ground in almost the same moment. The arrow made a slicing sound when it cut through the air.

"I am free!" Sabine yelled again. She lifted her hands above her head to show him. Another arrow came sailing through the open window, nicking the side of her neck.

She recoiled, stumbling to the side. The scent of her own blood filled the air, but she stared in horror at the fire raging behind her.

GARETH WASN'T GOING to let Sabine go.

Ruben turned and launched himself at Gareth who had joined

Ruben on the ground to watch the mill go up in flames. They went skidding back into the dirt, rolling and grappling. It was a fight for survival. Gareth snarled, wrapping his fingers around Ruben's throat.

"I am going to enjoy killing ye while yer woman burns," Gareth declared.

Ruben overcame the urge to try and loosen the grip on his neck. He curled his fingers in and flattened his hand. With his feet on the ground, he surged upwards and jabbed his clamped fist toward the spot directly beneath Gareth's ribs.

Gareth made a gurgling sound. Ruben tossed him to the side. Gareth hit the ground with a hard thud. He rolled over onto his back while struggling to draw breath.

Another arrow sliced through the air.

Ruben dived toward Gareth. He hooked his hands into the man, using him as a shield.

"I wonder if ye are still so very pleased with yer archer, Gareth." Ruben hooked his arm around Gareth's throat. The man struggled to draw in breath.

"Do ye...hear the...crackle...of the fire?" Gareth sputtered. "Go...save...yer...woman."

"I am saving her," Ruben said. "Neither of us will worry that ye will ever come back to trouble us in the future."

Gareth clawed desperately at Ruben's arm. He was fighting for his life.

But Ruben was fighting for the woman he loved. Which was more important than his own life.

Somewhere off to their right he heard men running. The night was brighter now, the fire growing large enough to alert the inhabitants of the stronghold. Escape would be impossible now. Everyone was running toward the fire.

Ruben let Gareth go.

Gareth rolled over, rising to one knee. Gareth clawed at the ground. He tried to rise, but his knees wouldn't hold him. So he crawled a few paces, dragging in huge breaths.

"Ye should...have...killed me...idiot," Gareth ground out. He turned his head, his teeth bared. "Now that I have the dowry and the Douglas joined with me...I am going to destroy yer clan!"

So passionate about his vision, Gareth pointed at Ruben while he stood. He smiled confidently, while his eyes glittered. Ruben heard the slice of the arrow cutting through the air. It hit Gareth in the chest, piercing through him.

He looked down at the point protruding from him. "No..."

A second arrow lodged in his belly.

"Archers can only hit what they see," Ruben muttered. "A larger target gains their attention first."

Gareth's eyes widened with understanding. He tried to say something, but his mouth was full of bright red blood. He drew in a last breath before falling backwards.

There was a strange rattle. A gust of wind seemed to come up from the very ground. It swirled around like a whip and then cracked, raising the dirt around Gareth's body. He contorted, his hands becoming claws.

And then he was gone.

Ruben felt it. As though some evil had just been taken to hell by the demons Gareth had always consorted with.

Ruben looked up but there was no way to know if the archers were still there.

Help me save her...

He finished his plea before turning and launching himself toward the burning workhouse. The back half had already been engulfed in flames.

People were coming but it would all be too late. He found the doors but there was a thick chain locked around the handles.

Gareth had never planned for Sabine to escape.

There had to be a way.

He looked around. Off to one side, a blacksmith's anvil was illuminated by the fire. Behind it there were tools hung up neatly.

Ruben grabbed an axe. He lifted it high before chopping at a wall that wasn't yet burning.

"Sabine!"

The axe cut through the wall. Smoke came pouring out. Ruben raised it again and again, chopping frantically until there was a hole.

Lindsey retainers finally arrived. They reached in to pull at the sides of the hole. Wood splintered. A wall of heat hit them all in the face. Ruben surged forward into the fire.

"Sabine!"

IT WAS TOO hot.

The doors were chained closed. Sabine struggled with a door, but it was no use. The air was becoming too thick to breathe. She wanted to try another door, but she was choking. Without air, her strength waned.

"Sabine!"

Her thoughts had grown fuzzy. She wanted to reply but coughed instead. Her knees crumpled. All around her the heat was growing more intense.

"Sweet Christ….at last."

Someone was nearby. Perhaps it was an angel. Sabine felt as if she was floating. Up, up and away from the swirling flames. The heat was left behind before she was lying down on crisp, cool grass.

"Sabine?"

Someone patted her cheeks.

"Come now, lass, we have a lifetime yet to share."

Was that Ruben? Was he dead too? Sabine found herself content with her fate. If Ruben was there too, they weren't parting.

A harder pat landed on her cheek. This one stung just a bit. Sabine frowned and opened her eyes. Ruben was staring down at her.

He was real.

Ruben clasped her tightly against his body, but Sabine wanted to be closer. She wrapped her arms around him, hugging him tightly.

"It's over, lass, ye are safe."

She felt his chest rumble. He stroked the back of her head before shifting and separating just enough so that he could look at her face.

"No one will ever dare hurt ye again," Ruben promised her. "We are getting married."

"Married?" Sabine realized there were numerous people around them. She wasn't the only one wondering about Ruben's announcement. He looked past her at someone.

"Who are ye, lass?" he asked.

"Gillan."

Sabine turned her head to see the girl was plucking at her skirt and looking miserable.

"I...didn't want to lie," Gillan sputtered. "But Gareth Gordon said he'd kill my mother if I did not do as he said."

"Gareth Gorden is dead," Ruben stated firmly. "He'll trouble no one ever again. Arland? Find out where the girl's mother is and bring her to Lindsey land."

"Ye are not putting me out?" Gillan's jaw hung open in astonishment.

"My lady wife to be would never allow it." Ruben returned his attention to Sabine. He helped her to her feet while the people around them returned to the task of keeping the fire from spreading. He held one of her hands in his. "Will ye marry me, Sabine?"

"I have no dowry."

"I want to wed ye, for yerself." Ruben grinned. "The Midnight Well has worked its magic on us both, lass. I am completely enchanted by ye."

A memory stirred of the first time they had met. Ruben cupped her jaw. "I love ye more than the breath in my body,

Sabine. As for the dowry, we'll make our way just fine. Yer knitting and my father's land. Let us leave the greed to the Gordons."

She smiled at him. There was no denying how happy his words made her. "I am not complete without you, Ruben. I will stay by your side for the rest of my life."

Their gazes were fused just as completely as their hearts were in that moment. The wind blew around them as if the very earth approved of their union. No ceremony could have been as binding.

His attention shifted to the Lindsey retainers standing behind her. His expression became tight. "I will make Sabine my wife before the sun sets tomorrow!"

He turned her away from him so that she was standing beside him. Shoulder to shoulder, they faced his clansmen as one. It was his solemn word, something the Lindsey retainers and the Hay retainers recognized. It was a binding oath older than Scotland. Honor was something that spanned the world with roots that ran deep into ancient times.

Eachan's lips split into a grin. He let out a loud "whoop." The others added their own cheers. They came toward Ruben and Sabine, gathering around them. The men offered their hands to Ruben. He clasped their wrists, a smile on his face.

Dugan Hay was the last. "Now this is fine news I will be able to take home to Braylin."

"Let's go home, lass," Ruben said.

Home. Sabine lifted her chin, so happy, it felt as if she was glowing like a full moon. Ahead of her was a life rich with hope. The only thing that truly mattered was that Ruben was with her. Together, they'd build a future full of happiness.

And if she were enchanted by the Midnight Well, she hoped she never recovered!

Oisin's study—

"FATHER?" RUBEN HELD a candle up.

"Come in," Oisin grunted. "Arland has already told ye I am here." His father looked up at him. "Deny it, and I will call ye ten kinds of a fool for leaving yer bed when ye have such a fine partner sharing it with ye."

"He did tell me ye were down here before first light," Ruben admitted. "What concerns ye?"

"Would ye worry about me sanity if I admitted that inside, I am still the young man I was at yer age?" Oisin asked. He tapped an open letter in front of him. "Yet it's true that age has taken a toll on me. It's here. Clearly written. Neilina Douglas is 17 and has her mother's blonde hair. I should have realized the girl was not yer bride."

"I should have checked as well." Ruben took the letter, reading it twice before he shook his head.

His father indulged in a few chuckles. "Well now. Matters have resolved themselves rather well. Very fine timing too. I will see ye married to yer May Day Queen and none too soon. The lass has nae bled since she arrived."

"How would ye know such a detail?" Ruben was aghast.

Laird Lindsey merely raised a white eyebrow. "Do nae begrudge me such knowledge, son. My days are numbered. Before I go, I wanted to know if there was new life sprouting here. And so it has."

Oisin flattened his hand on the desktop firmly.

"But let the little lass tell ye later. She'll likely enjoy being wed before she realizes yer seed has taken root."

His father had a bright smile on his face. His eyes glittered with renewed spirit. He pointed with one gnarled finger at one of the cabinets. "Now there is a wee bit of scotch over there. I've been saving it for just the right moment. Let's toast to me first grandchild."

꘎꘎꘎꘎

SABINE WOKE EARLY.

She lay still for a moment, wondering just why she was so alert. Her belly heaved, nausea hitting her hard.

She fought against the bedding, succeeding in getting her feet untangled just in time. Her belly was heaving. She made it to the garderobe just in time.

It didn't make any sense to be so violently ill with nothing in her belly. Sabine sat on her knees, her body quivering slightly while she pondered what ailed her.

Looking across the chamber, she saw Ruben's spare shirt. So simple an item but it was precious because it was proof of his devotion to her. Sabine felt her eyes widen with understanding.

Her mother was always sick in the mornings when she was newly with child. The small home the Hawlyn family lived in on the border didn't afford her mother any privacy. Sabine had heard her mother retching at daybreak just half a year before.

Sabine laid a protective hand over her belly.

She was suddenly full of joy. It was so bright; she couldn't stay still. She hurried to dress, wrinkling her nose at the drab dress. She wanted to celebrate, and she whirled around on her way to the door.

She had to tell Ruben.

And Oisin.

It seemed that Laird Lindsey would be getting what he'd wished for. Her belly would grow large and round throughout the growing season. Her joy doubled.

It was still very early. There were a few people stirring but Sabine was surprised to see Gillan already coming down the steps.

"Gillan? It is very early," Sabine said.

Gillian hadn't seen her just yet. The girl turned her head and smiled at Sabine. She held something up. "I did it."

Sabine closed the distance between them. In Gillian's hands

was a piece of sample knitting. The girl had successfully learned to do the most basic stitch on four needles. There was much yet to learn but the girl showed promise.

"So you have," Sabine praised the girl. "The stitches are nice and even. You will be knitting on silver wires before you know it."

Gillan nodded. "I will practice more than any of the others. Ye shall see. I am going to learn a trade."

Gillian's face was full of determination. She flashed Sabine a smile before she headed off toward the kitchen. Something moved at the end of the passageway. Sabine watched as Arland came closer. He contemplated her for a moment.

"Ye have the makings of a fine mistress," Arland stated.

It was high praise. Sabine felt it warm her insides. But a scent came out of the kitchen. Her belly instantly knotted and started to heave. Sabine dashed away before she ended up retching in front of the captain.

CHAPTER EIGHTEEN

F EBRUARY WAS A bitter month.

The wind howled down from the north. Everything was frozen and had been so for too long. The necessities of daily life were harder because of the need to open doors.

But no one in the Lindsey stronghold cared about the weather. They were clustered around the hearth in the great hall. A gaggle of younger boys were set to stand watch near the opening to the passageway. They took to their duty with firm expressions.

Norrie came down the steps, her pace quick. She looked at the boys and shook her head before she dashed into the kitchen. When she returned, she carried a kettle. There was steam rising from it. Norrie held it away from her body and took to the stairs once again.

Several women were inside Ruben's chamber.

"Ye are doing well. Bear with it."

Sabine leaned over, gripping the back of a birthing chair. It was a good thing the piece of furniture was sturdy because she needed support. Another pain began. It moved around her hips from front to back. But the moment it passed, sitting became intolerable. Sabine was up, walking around the chamber because it was the only thing that made the pain bearable.

"Breathe. Deep breath now," the midwife instructed as the woman kept pace beside her.

The door to the chamber opened, allowing a wonderfully cool rush of air to hit Sabine. In naught but her smock, she should have been cold, but she was dripping sweat.

Well, it is called labor…

Sabine agreed with her inner voice. It was hard work to give birth to a child. The intensity built until the pains came nearly on top of one another. The women who had insisted on being in the chamber were now very welcome because they guided her to the birthing chair.

"There it is…I see the head…push hard…" the midwife instructed firmly.

It all felt like too much. Too much pain, too much pressure. But there was also an instinct stirring inside of her. Sabine gripped the arm rest of the chair and put all of her energy into pushing her child into the world.

In one moment, she felt the baby move. The women watching leaned in to see the baby. The midwife rubbed the infant. Everyone held their breath, waiting for a sign of life.

"Come on now." The midwife rubbed vigorously. "There are so many people waiting to meet ye."

Sabine felt a lump rising in her throat. But in that moment when dread was starting to fill her, the baby stiffened. It raised its arms and legs before letting out a wail.

A murmur of relief sounded around her. The midwife nodded. "That's the way, my wee little one."

The baby shuddered. It drew in a deeper breath and let out a cry that was loud enough to bounce off the chamber walls. Everyone smiled while the midwife swaddled the child.

"Ye have a daughter, mistress."

The midwife laid the baby in Sabine's arms. In that moment she was sure that she learned a whole new meaning of the word love. For months she had known a child was growing inside of her. She'd expected to love it. But the emotion that filled her was so much greater than any she had ever felt before.

Well, except for the love she had for Ruben.

That was a love that had filled her completely until now. Now there was even more room in her heart, the tiny little new life in her arms filling her even fuller.

A lifetime would be too short.

OISIN WAS WAITING in the great hall as well.

"They're coming!" one of the younger lads called out.

"I hear the baby!" another boy added on his way down the aisle toward the head table.

A collective sigh of relief rippled through the hall in response to the news that the baby was alive. Stern expressions eased and smiles of anticipation brightened the faces of those waiting.

Everyone turned to watch Morven enter the hall. She smiled radiantly, a small bundle in her arms.

"Shhhh...quiet down..." Arland ordered.

The hall grew silent enough to hear the wind howling on the other side of the closed window shutters. In sharp contrast to the winter storm, the baby let out a soft coo. The maids sighed and the retainers grinned.

Morven made her way to the head table.

"Ye have a fine granddaughter, laird." Morven handed the baby to Ruben.

Ruben took the infant, a slightly uncertain look appearing on his face. Morven gently taught him the way of holding the baby. The child let out another little gurgle once Ruben had her cradled in his arms.

Oisin leaned over to look at the baby. He stuck out his pinky so she could curl her little fingers around it.

"She is perfect," Laird Lindsey announced jubilantly. He looked up to find that people were waiting to see what he thought of the child's gender.

"The Lindseys are blessed to have a fine, healthy girl born today. Me granddaughter is most welcome. Very welcome indeed! She shall be named Caire Ann. For she is very beloved."

A ripple of approval went through the room.

"Allision? Gillan? Come and meet yer cousin."

Allision was happy to do as her father instructed. Gillan held back, clearly uncertain. Allision turned around and grabbed Gillan by the hand. "Come. Ye are part of our family, as we have told ye. I will even let ye hold Caire Ann before me to prove it."

Gillan brightened up. "Really?"

"Yes, really!"

"Go and see yer wife, son," Oisin muttered softly. "She has brought a great and welcome blessing to this house. To the Lindsey. Tell her I said so."

Ruben carefully took his daughter from Gillan. Morven watched him carefully while he secured the baby in his arms once more. The Lindsey stretched their necks and leaned in to get a glimpse of the child when Ruben passed. By the time he made it into the passageway, someone had started playing music.

Aye, it was time to celebrate.

Ruben felt as if the very air inside the stronghold was once again full of life and promise. Life would always be challenging, but so long as they had hope, they would face the future together.

It was a future that promised to be full of love.

Rake Hell
1556

IT WAS FINE and warm now. June 23 marked the middle of the growing season and St. John's Eve. Temperance drew in a deep breath and let it out. The fine weather made her long to strip her linen modesty cap off her head. But her family's Puritan devotion forbade her to do so.

She was so tired of shall'nt's.

Life seemed to be nothing but a list of things she could not do. Both of her sisters were held as examples of what happened to women who failed to be obedient.

Obedient…

There was another thing she was sick unto death of.

Was not joy part of a good life?

"Temperance?"

Her mother called from the front room of the home they lived in. Although "hid in" was a better way to phrase it. They were in hiding because Temperance's father refused to obey the new queen's law to return to the Catholic faith.

Temperance felt a chill go down her spine. There were soldiers in the village now. No one spoke of the matter, but she knew in her heart that those men might arrive to take them all away to trial. They no longer ventured into the village because Puritans were not welcome. People feared that if they were seen with those defying the royal order, they might be swept away into prison along with the Puritans.

"Temperance?"

"Yes mother?"

Her mother appeared in the doorway between the kitchen and the outer room. Her mother was worrying her lower lip.

Temperance finished drying a bowl while her mother continued to debate whatever she was thinking of asking. Finally, her mother sighed.

"The cow broke through the fence. Your father and brothers have gone to mend it. They must also find the other cows...." Her mother's attention strayed to the window. The shutters were closed now because the sun had set.

The night and those who cast spells under its dark cloak were strictly shut out of their home. Both of her sisters had gone out into the night, and they were gone now.

Temperance was suddenly warmed by the possibility of doing something forbidden. It wasn't that she craved recklessness, but the night was warm and fine. Washing dishes wasn't exciting in the least.

"What would you have me do, mother?" Temperance asked directly. She folded her hands in front of her, trying to appear calm. But her heart was thumping hard with anticipation.

To go outside beneath the summer sky. There would be starlight and moonlight...oh and it was St. John's Eve too. Bonfires would be burning.

"The hens escaped. Since they have recently been fed, they are not returning. I fear the foxes will get them in the night. They are likely in the meadow." Her mother's hand was resting on her distended belly. Another child would be born within the month.

"I will go," Temperance assured her mother.

Temperance began to head toward the side door of the kitchen. Her mother caught her forearm. "Remember your sisters' downfall, Temperance. Do not be tempted by the night wind."

Concern was etched deeply into her mother's face. Guilt stirred inside of her for being so eager to get into the night. Temperance covered her mother's hand with her own. "Thank you for reminding me, mother."

Temperance loved her mother. It was a cruel twist of fate to have her parents so devoted to the Puritan faith. Cruel because inside of her, Temperance wasn't calm or obedient at all.

No, she heard the music blowing in the night breeze. All the trees had their summer coats of leaves. They rustled with an invitation, calling to her to come out and dance beneath the moonlight. She felt as if she was bursting with the need to celebrate being alive instead of huddling in her burrow too frightened to poke her head out.

Hiding wasn't living.

Somewhere up on the hills there would be bonfires tonight to celebrate the height of the warm season. People would jump over the fires for good luck. Her older sisters had gone to the Samhain bonfires. Now they were both gone, and her mother feared Temperance would follow.

She couldn't break her mother's heart.

Temperance drew in a breath and let out a sigh. The wind blew again, this time the clouds parted, permitting the stars to illuminate the meadow. Flowers were still in bloom, making a very enchanted setting.

Picking a few flowers wasn't going to break her mother's heart.

Nor would muttering the traditional St. John's Day rhyme.

"Blossom...sweet blossom...the first that I have found..." Temperance paused with her fingertips gently resting on the delicate petals of a flower, "...in the name of Jesus Christ, I pluck it from the ground..." she snapped the stem with a little twist, "...as Joseph loved sweet Mary...and took her for wife without fear..." snap, snap, snap, snap, "...so, in a dream this night..." snap, "...I hope my true love will appear." Snap.

Seven flowers.

Temperance held them in one hand, happily pleased with her little whimsy. Above her, the clouds shifted. Moonlight illuminated the flowers. Temperance felt her breath catch for the moon was bright and full. She tipped her head back to admire it.

A full moon.

Temperance looked at the well. It stood at the top of the meadow. Known as the Midnight Well, it was rumored to be enchanted.

Her sister Prudence had gone there beneath a full moon to seek a glimpse of her true love. Tonight was St. John's Eve, the night when the fae folk were the most powerful.

But there would be no forest fruit to eat just yet.

Temperance frowned. But not for long. She brightened up because it was St. John's Eve. So she could go and wash her hands and face in the water of the enchanted midnight well to wash away bad luck. It was only a slight twisting of the legend. And on this night, perhaps the fae folk might look kindly upon her. Somehow show her a future with love and in a place where she might still embrace her mother.

She tucked the flowers into her cleavage for safekeeping. The moonlight was so bright, she had ample light to see a path up to the well. Something else caught her eye. Bright and round, she felt herself compelled to kneel down and discover just what it was.

It was a strawberry.

Plump and bright red. Several more were scattered over the meadow among the flowers. She plucked one and then another. When her hand was full, she lifted them to her face so she could inhale their sweet scent.

There was nothing like summer berries!

The scent combined with the flowers in her cleavage. Summer with all of its wonder filled her to the brim in that moment.

She headed up to the enchanted well. Temperance tossed the strawberries into her mouth so that she might pull up a bucket of water. Their sweet taste filled her mouth, making her smile. The rope became wet, glistening in the starlight. When she saw the bucket, the moonlight broke through and showed down onto the water filling it.

And the face of a man who was leaning over the other side of the well.

"Sweet Mercy!" Temperance exclaimed.

He chuckled at her. "I did wonder what words might escape your lips if I startled you." He clicked his tongue. "I'd hoped for something more...explicit."

Temperance sat the bucket on the edge of the well. Her heart was thumping away inside of her chest, but it wasn't from fear. Somehow, she knew that what was agitating her wasn't that emotion at all.

No, it was something altogether different.

"Jasper Hardwin." Temperance recalled his identity from May Day morning a year and a half past.

He performed a reverence with a little flourish of his hand. "I am flattered to know you recall my name."

"You should not be," Temperance informed him. "For I recall very well that you are also a Rakehell."

The sound of him chuckling floated across the opening of the well. A new emotion rippled through her. Something that hinted at a very deep enjoyment of standing up to him.

"Come now, mistress," Jasper teased her and started to come

around the well toward her. "I can hear in your voice how excited you are."

"What arrogance, sir," Temperance chastised him. "I am not here looking for you."

"And yet...." he took another step around the well toward her, "...here I am. A much more stimulating question is...what will you do when I venture closer to you?"

He held his position, leaving her feeling suspended between heartbeats.

She caught one corner of his mouth just starting to twitch up. It heralded his intention to move. Jasper jumped to one side, but she was ready and nimbly evaded his advance. They ended up trading places with the well still between them.

Temperance hiked her skirts up higher. She was poised on the edge of anticipation. Breathless.

Jasper raised an eyebrow toward her. This time, he rocked back and forth, leaning to one side and then to the other and back again. She watched him, trying to decide where he would go. She heard his foot hit the ground hard. The sound spurred her into action, only he was faking.

Temperance bolted straight into his arms.

He caught her, spinning around and around while she tried to recoil.

He was so hard. His chest. His arms. All of them were solid and firm.

And she liked it.

His embrace made her head spin. By the time he stopped, she was clinging to him because he was the only solid thing for her to cling to. Their gazes were locked. She saw an answering flicker of excitement in his eyes.

The clouds above them shifted, obscuring the moon. Darkness closed around them like the window shutters being closed. Temperance discovered her senses intensifying now that her sight wasn't keen.

She drew in a breath and noticed what Jasper smelled like.

The scent traveled into her lungs and then deeper into her flesh, setting off a new awareness of him. One that came with impulses. Her fingertips had grown more sensitive. She caught herself spreading her fingers out so that she might brush her fingertips across the hard surface of his chest.

The wind blew harder now, causing all of the trees to rustle like a thousand witnesses gossiping about what she and Jasper were doing.

Temperance stiffened. She felt her eyes widen. "We must stop."

"I suppose you are correct, mistress," Jasper muttered in a bare whisper. "Shall I confess that I do not want to stop?"

His question confounded her. But then she recalled that he was a self-confessed Rake Hell.

"My parents have warned me to not have dealings with men such as you."

"I wonder, dear lady...just who are your words meant for? Me or yourself?" Jasper asked in a wicked whisper.

He released her, leaving her standing alone with his words echoing inside her head.

"No rebuke?" Jasper inquired after a moment. He flattened his hand over his chest. "Careful, mistress, I might see an invitation in your lack of reprimand."

"The only reprimand I have is for myself," Temperance muttered. "For clinging to you."

She hadn't really thought her answer through. The words simply came out of her like a confession. She felt exposed and realized that she wanted to see what he'd do.

Would he try to exploit her weakness for him?

That was what Rake Hells did, or so her parents would say. As for herself, he was her very first true encounter with a Rake Hell.

So far...you are tempted...

Jasper stepped up close to her again. He was so close, her skirt hem brushed the top of his boots. So close that their breath mingled. Temperance discovered herself raising her chin so that their gazes remained locked.

She was captivated by him.

"You shouldn't toy with me," Jasper muttered. "I might take advantage of you."

"You won't," Temperance retorted.

"That is a very dangerous gamble, mistress."

Jasper was warning her. Temperance knew it and yet, venturing closer to the flames she saw in his eyes was all she wanted to do. He reached out, stroking one of her cheeks with the back of his finger.

The contact between their skin made her shudder. It was more than just a shiver for she felt the vibration all the way to her core. He drew in a stiff breath and retreated.

"I concede the victory to you tonight."

He was gone a second later, like he'd materialized from the darkness and just melted back into it. Temperance felt him all around her.

But the truth was, her awareness of him was inside of her. Discarding it would be impossible.

Jasper Hardwin would be lurking in her dreams.

To be continued in Rake Hell, a Mary Wine novel.

About the Author

Mary Wine has written over twenty novels that take her readers from the pages of history to the far reaches of space. Recent winner of a 2008 EPPIE Award for erotic western romance, her book LET ME LOVE YOU was quoted "Not to be missed…" by Lora Leigh, New York Times best-selling author.

When she's not abusing a laptop, she spends time with her sewing machines…all of them! Making historical garments is her second passion. From corsets and knickers to court dresses of Elizabeth I, the most expensive clothes she owns are hundreds of years out of date. She's also an active student of martial arts, having earned the rank of second degree black belt.

Milton Keynes UK
Ingram Content Group UK Ltd.
UKHW021917201124
451474UK00013B/794